# A
# DIAMOND
## OF
# DUST

## MY STORY, HIS GLORY

*"He died that I may live to tell my tale."*

**A. ANATO SWU**

Published by
Maurice Wylie Media
Bethel Media House
Tobermore
Magherafelt
Northern Ireland
BT45 5SG (UK)

Publisher's statement: Throughout this book the love for our God is such that whenever we
refer to Him we honour with Capitals. On the other hand, when referring to the devil, we
refuse to acknowledge him with any honour to the point of violating grammatical rule and
withholding capitalisation.

DISCLAIMER
The information contained in this book is not intended nor implied to be a substitute for
professional medical diagnosis or medical advice, or a licensed physician. It is provided for
educational purposes only.
You assume full responsibility for how you choose to use this information.

For more information visit
www.MauriceWylieMedia.com

*DEDICATED TO...*
*My beloved Dad, Mum, sister and brothers.*

# *Contents*

# *Acknowledgements*

My greatest acknowledgement is to God alone, for who I am today is because of what the Lord WAS, IS, and WILL BE; forever faithful and never changing. Thank you Almighty God for Your 'Gift of Love" and this 'New Life in Christ'. Truly You, are the 'God of New beginnings' and the 'God of the Second Chance.'

Thank you, my dear Mum for your unwavering faith and belief; and for instilling hope and confidence in your son when everything else seemed lost. Your tears carried on the wings of prayer are one of the few reasons why Heaven chose to give me a second chance. May God bless and bring you safely and healthily to the day when you will wholeheartedly and joyously enter His presence.

The life and testimony of certain people are like a lamp for multitudes travelling in the dark. I am honoured to mention here Maurice Wylie, and his esteemed lady wife (Mama) Maureen Wylie, who brought back 'light and love' into my life. This book has been made possible because of their immense love and concern for some aimless soul half a world away. Their desire to publish my story for wider reach and distribution sprung in me a sincere will to rewrite afresh the entire first edition print. May your effort and dedication win many souls for God and may your relentless service and sacrificial work towards the extension of His kingdom gather for you treasures in Heaven.

Mention should be made of those people who have been providing me with the urge and inspiration to be a better person through their constructive criticisms.

I wish to thank my only sister, Aghali Swu for her constant support and encouragement.

My acknowledgement would remain incomplete if I failed to mention Henivi Prayer Centre. It is indisputably one of the most intriguing and miracle-filled prayer centres in the world. I literally would not be writing this book had I not experienced the miracle in my drug-trapped, hopeless life from the centre.

Thank you, Pastor Luvukhu, counsellors, and all prayer warriors.

*Anato*

# *Foreword*

When I was asked to read this book at first, my natural judgement kicked in. Was this another medical student's attempt at a clinical text book, to warn about the dangers of drugs?

Instead I was faced with a glimpse of true reality. A sobering account of life with addiction from both a personal and family perspective.

This book throws down a challenge not just to those in addiction or helping someone with addiction, it also challenges the heart of the Christian who works in the field.

I have worked with addiction and suicide for the past 11 years, both inside and outside faith circles. I have seen how God has showed up in the lives of an addict, but I have also witnessed how this world provides them with the excuse not to follow through with God.

The author leads you down a number of polarising paths that clash against the known stereotyped life. He moulds the picture of his life story with twists and turns that challenge your understanding of addiction. There is a seemingly uncovering of an underbelly that no one wishes to unveil or accept its existence.

Anato Swu, once a stable university medical student, becomes qualified in a doctorate of life. As an unravelling sequence of what seems like an unending cycle of addiction, shame and disappointments hit him.

Then, like Saul on the Road to Damascus, God became very real to him and a spiritual journey started to unfold. But even as a young

Christian in the Lord, suicidal thoughts would still haunt and challenge him to end his life. It was at this point that God gave a vision to a person from 'Half A World Away', showing them the struggles and desperation that Anato was facing, which led to a remarkable testimony of God's Unconditional Love and Sovereign Grace.

There have been books published previously that tell of an addict's story; and books designed to help the addict through their difficult withdrawal periods, but this book takes you on a journey through the why's. Dealing with a hidden lifestyle and the internal turmoil of an addict whose only way out was to contemplate suicide, this book will take you on an emotional journey and help you understand how drugs and alcohol abuse can lead one down a path of destruction. Written very sympathetically, it describes the impact of suffering that the families endure but most importantly it tells us that no matter how far into the depths of despair that an addict finds him or herself, there is One who can transform their life, and that is our Lord Jesus Christ.

Without any doubt, I can unreservedly recommend this book to any person who is addicted to substance abuse, or family who has a loved one addicted. This book would be an excellent resource to churches or charities that seek to reach those who have been affected by drug addiction or suicide.

**James E Scott**
*Community Pastor, New Life City Church*
*Community Development Worker*
*Drug and Alcohol Community Support Worker*
*Conference and Workshop Speaker*

# *Prologue*

Throughout the world, drug and alcohol addiction are major problems for many families, communities and law enforcement. They cause harm far beyond the physical and psychological health of the addict and are associated with serious social and developmental issues. Reiterating the fact, the World Drug Report released by the United Nations Office on Drugs and Crime (UNODC) on June 22, 2017, that roughly 5% of the world population abused drugs at least once during the past few years. In addition, an estimated 0.6% of the global adult population was addicted to narcotic drugs; 'the effects of which call for imminent treatment'.

The Guardian reported that an annual snapshot of drug use says that out of 230 million people, one in every twenty took illicit drugs at least once in 2010. There are about 27 million problem drug users, mainly chronic heroin or cocaine users, representing about 0.6% of the world's population.[1]

Addiction is more common than you think! Out of 24 million Americans who have used illicit drugs in the preceding month, 19.6 million have had substance abuse disorder in the preceding year. One in 10 Americans has a drug abuse problem.[2]

Within the UK, around 1 in 12 (8.4%) of adults aged 16 to 59 had taken a drug in the last year. This is around 2.7 million people.[3]

While World Health Organisation estimates a whopping 2 billion people across the world consume alcoholic drinks.[4]

## *Alcohol*

The harmful use of alcohol results in 3.3 million deaths each year. On average each person in the world aged 15 years of age, drinks 6.2 litres of alcohol per year. Less than half the population (38.3%) actually drinks alcohol, this means that those who do drink it consume on average 17 litres of alcohol annually.

## *Drugs*

Some 31 million people have drug use disorders. Almost 11 million people inject drugs, of which 1.3 are living with HIV, 5.5 million with Hepatitis C, and 1 million with both HIV and Hepatitis C.[5]

It's reported in my own country of India, that there are over three million drug addicts with an increase in the use of prescription drugs. The most commonly used drugs are, cannabis, heroin, opium and hashish, with increasing prevalence of methamphetamine. In some countries the drugs are smuggled and marked illegally, and it includes a broad spectrum of marijuana (ganja), brown sugar (a form of heroin), LSD, and prescription drugs, which I would rather not present at this time.

This grim revelation of facts and figures shows how far the unseen tentacles of drugs and alcohol addiction have spread across the entire world, far beyond our imagination. Even to the point where drug addicts actually staged a protest in 1999 in Nagaland, due to the price hike of drug purchases.

It was only a number of years ago, if people had been caught with drugs they would have been marked as an outcast of the community, but now with diminishing morals, easy availability and lax policing, we have accepted 'drug dealers' as part of the community. What was abnormal to our communities and schools have now become norm, sad to say.

I am only too aware that the drug hazard knows no bounds. From the non-schooled to the highly educated; from the jobless to the Government officials; from the Primary School students to the granny... many are becoming addicted to drugs. The sadness is, before long that menace could come knocking on your family circle door, if not already. But why wait? When today you can arm yourself with the knowledge of how to guard your loved ones, and if required; lead them to a path of wholeness again?

## Lost Hope & Faith

*Behold, why'd I still be alive,*
*When to live, I no longer strive?*
*Why'd the sun still shine,*
*Upon this poor soul of mine?*

*Oh! Can't anybody hear me*
*Or this tattered life see?*
*Oh! Won't someone rescue me,*
*Before eternally damned I be?*

*Know ye not the end is near?*
*Know ye not, soon I won't be there?*
*How late find me this life so dear,*
*After it's consumed by tears and fear.*

*Here now, on the 'morrow ye'd search.*
*Too late! The casket's in the Church.*
*Forever gone, sans bidding even a bye,*
*Leaving thee alone to ponder on why!*

*By Anato*
*(Composed as an Addict)*

# *Introduction*

Drug abuse, and its elder brother alcoholism, is nothing but the devil's death plan on an instalment basis into the lives of people. Seldom does one ever hear about a person who died within a few days or months after having taken up these self-harming, anti-social habits.

The reason for this is because the devil makes sure to take a little piece of your body and soul, every time you allow 'these evil brothers' to abuse you; and he smirks over every single shot or peg you willingly (in) take.  Finally, he laughs in all his evil glory when you are totally consumed and wasted; another taken down by deception.

People experiment with drugs and alcohol for different reasons. Many first try out of curiosity; because of peer-pressure (to be accepted among groups or for friend's sake); to gain confidence; to ease another problem (anxiety, stress, depression) or to enhance athletic performance. In other cases, it can be the seeking of a companion to fill a void.  Once you become addicted to any or both (rare but not uncommon), it becomes a complex disorder characterised by compulsive use.

The repeated use causes impaired judgement, inability to think clearly, abnormal behaviour and feelings. The uncontrollable craving to use drugs and/or alcohol becomes more important than anything else, including your own health, happiness, family, friends and career.

As addiction takes hold, your health and job performance progressively deteriorate; you may miss or frequently be late for work or school/ college and you start to neglect social or family obligations. Bad time-keeping and negligence within the work force become more regular than not.

In your mind the onus will never be yours; it's always someone else's fault. But in truth, this is the addiction manifesting into a character defect which is denied by the addict. Your ability to stop using is mentally compromised. What began then as a voluntary choice by exercising free will given by God, has now turned into physical and psychological need. If the addiction continues, then you may well be assured that the death sentence passed on your first day of wilful abuse will take effect very soon in the form of a premature, undignified death.

There is no guaranteed medical cure for drug/alcohol addiction, although scientific research may prescribe and proclaim otherwise. Medical treatment and recovery are a long process that often experiences setbacks. Relapses occur in the majority of drug abusers who are declared cured from rehabilitation centres.

Some of the addicts become even more abusive and aggressive users than they had before treatment, switching to different drugs or methods, and while the same may not be said for alcoholics, there are many possible chances of relapses. The only guaranteed cure for any type of addiction is through the power of Jesus Christ. It may take a very long time for you to realise and try out this free course, it could be because you still love abusing stuffs, or you have lost all your hopes and faith and totally surrendered yourself in the hands of satan. But, it doesn't take long to be cured wholly and completely if you take your addictive nature to the merciful God, as Scripture states, *'The things which are impossible with men are possible with God.'* Luke 18:27

For spiritual healing and restoration, the only things you need are a desire to give up, the will to repent and confess, seek forgiveness from God and ask the Holy Spirit to help you. Soon the process of healing will begin, and getting cured completely may not take even a week! If I, with over 20 years drug and alcohol abuse can, I believe so can you!

CHAPTER 1

# *The story you will not hear...*

It was during my third semester at medical school that things really escalated. I was studying for a Bachelor of Medicine and a Bachelor of Surgery in the top medical school in India. Before I started my studies, I was just a typical young man growing up in a cultural society, but through bad choices and wrong company, I slowly became someone I didn't recognise.

It was the end of term, I was leaving school and going back to my home town in Nagaland to spend the break with my family. When I arrived home, I would greet my family warmly, however afterwards I would quickly go to my room and remain there. During that time, I chose to keep myself confined in my room because my drug addictive nature found no real joy or peace in the company of other family members.

I had started abusing drugs socially and on my own but now secretively, I was even doing it at home. I sat on my bed and pondered hard on what I had made out of my once-cherished life.

Here I was, a prestige student, aspiring to become a top surgeon, my parents sacrificing their life of enjoyment to pay me through the premier institute of Andhra Medical College, in India. Yet my biggest concern was when I couldn't find a vein in my body to inject another dose of Morphine or Valium.

It wasn't that I didn't know where my veins were; as I had spent my first two years learning it in anatomy class as a medical student, but because of the amount I was injecting myself, my veins were now collapsing. In fact, some had already stopped functioning.

My body had out-drunk itself from all types of hard core drink. My blood was rejecting the injected drugs due to the amount of abuse I had allowed the blood cells to suffer. I had no other option left than to take the drugs orally and watch and feel my entire body decay gradually. My limbs were grossly enlarged and my legs in particular!

I made sure that my family were occupied with other things, so around lunchtime, I locked myself into my bedroom for privacy and I began to search for veins. I had to give up in frustration when I couldn't find even a single small vein to fix my drug-hungry system with a drug solution chemical that was available at the time as a popular substance of abuse.

I was really annoyed as I had just spent so much time grounding the contents of the capsules and dissolving it in a few millilitres of distilled water. I loved that time of excitement as I drained the dissolved chemical with a syringe, using a small ball of cotton as a filter, knowing what was coming next.

In anticipation of a euphoric high, I had removed my belt and tied it on my left arm. Just as a vein popped up, I plunged the needle into it, but immediately I had to pull out the syringe. There was no blood flowing in the vein! It had collapsed. I tried it on my other arm with the same result.

I sat for a few minutes feeling such frustration and annoyance at myself and my useless body. I wasn't giving up though, I removed my trousers, took out a neck-tie from my drawer, and tied it around my leg above the ankle joint. A few veins popped up and I tried to inject the drug solution but it didn't work. I felt despair.

After 12 years of secret abuse all my visible veins had collapsed or were collapsing. I took out another strip. I removed its covering and washed down all eight of the capsules in one go with a glass of water and lay on my bed impatiently waiting for the drugs to take effect.

Towards that evening, the effect of the drugs had almost worn off, so I gently moved off the bed where my exhausted and drugged body had fallen asleep and hearing my family's voices in the next room, reminded me of how much I had let them down. The star of their family was a drunkard and a druggie who saw only misery and grief around him, and no longer had any hope. The lifeboat of rescue was not to be found.

I bolted the door from within and made my mind up to end it all. My drug-influenced mind had finally concluded that my family members, who were the most affected and deeply anguished by my drug addiction, would no longer suffer heartaches if I end my life.

As I sat deep in thought, I looked for my rope, that I had made up with strips of sheet tied together. This rope was one that I had pulled out many times from my wardrobe to look at. It was some form of security that I could end the pain at any time.

I found myself pondering again at it, thinking it would enable me to exit this world without much hassle or tension, and be free of pain and depression.

Standing on my tiptoes, I stretched up to the beam that hung across the end of my bed and tied the rope tightly. Placing my head into the other end of the rope I could hear the laughs of my family members, they were not aware of what was unfolding in their own home.

Looking around the room one last time, I saw the tried and tested drugs, empty gelatin capsules and cigarette butts, the empty bottle of drink, and the syringes which I had kept hidden within the room when not in use.

I looked over to see the family photo that sat beside my bed one last time. My life was about to end. I was going to step off my bed in a moment and be no more! As I tightened the noose around my neck and lowered my feet getting ready to step off the bed, I began to choke, cough and sob.

My family heard the unusual noises and Aghali my sister, rushed to my door calling out aloud… "Anato! Anato! Anato!" I remained silent for a time then loosened the noose and also the other end of the rope and hid it. With no response from me, Aghali burst into the room and as she did, I saw her eyes widen in shock at the sight before her.

For many who read this book, suicide is an option that they keep close to their chest. It's that last card they can play when the deal has gone sour in life. What I never realised is what happens after that last card has been played for those whom we love? Consider this, it is painful for those who love us to have an addicted family member, but what is more painful than an addicted family member… a dead family member.

Keeping in perspective of what families suffer when an act of suicide takes place, I have taken the liberty to let my sister share in her own words about that day she burst through my bedroom door.

# *Aghali's account...*

I have always considered my brother Anato to be wise, strong, confident, and without any bad habits, but what I discovered on that particular night would change my belief, and my opinion of his personality and character completely!

When I burst into the room, Anato was wiping the tears from his eyes and sitting on the end of the bed. The room was in a mess. There were syringes and empty bottles of alcohol laying around the room.

I stood there in shock and asked him, "What were you doing?"

He simply replied, "Nothing!" He then went silent. This was now his normal attitude, gone were the days of the bright, cheerful brother I once had. Knowing he was closed down in his mind, I knew it would be a futile attempt to coax out any answer from him that night. So, I also sat down in silence and pretended nothing too serious had happened while my heart ached and my mind failed to register any sense or wisdom.

I was looking around the room when I noticed the end of a rope hanging out of a drawer, as if someone had tried to hide it. It was then I realised, he had tried to commit suicide using the rope and must have panicked hearing me trying to get into the room. My heart ached in unbearable pain.

After a few tense moments he left the room giving me the chance to take his rope and hide it in a place where he would not find it.

It was then I told my parents about the incident. Immediately, they hastened to my brother's room and noticed that he was not sober, so they didn't talk to him, instead, they prayed for him.

That night I sat on the seat in the corner of my brother's room, and staying awake all night watching over him as he slept soundly. My grieving heart was broken, I realised that if I hadn't of burst through the door, we could all have been planning his funeral.

Tears of sadness would run that night from me for a brother I loved with every part of my heart.

The next morning my brother would awaken to begin his new day, but he would have forgotten most of the things that occurred the previous night, but the hearts of those who loved him were now broken in despair, how, if ever, were we going to see my brother made whole?

For many people who knows little, or nothing at all, about drugs or substance abuse, this is like an alien story. However, to those who have a family member who is a drug addict, or an addict themselves, this story may not garner much appreciation, or surprise, only sympathy and comfort to the bereaved or the affected family.

However, left unsaid and unshared, this story wouldn't instil fear and insecurities in the mind of the addict who would start wondering, *'who'd be the next me?'* The same thought would overwhelm those families with drug-addicted members and the question thus, 'who among the family members will be next?'

This is the part when one's body is found hung or slumped over a chair, a needle/syringe lying next to them. The parent or friend comes home, to find the police in your home and informs them that you have passed away. The relation breaks down uncontrollably... their last hope for you has been dashed; the one that they give birth will, in a few hours' time, be buried. Your days as a mortal is over and the sun, moon and the stars will not show their face to you. You will be seen and felt for the last time.

Your sister or brother asks the question when can they see you? The response is one they never would have anticipated. A police officer says, "You cannot see them yet. An autopsy has to be carried out." You're now a scene of an investigation!

I want you to understand what we do to ourselves does not just affect us but those around us. Just take a minute and think about those who smile in love at you, those who appreciate you. That person who smiles and appreciates you that will be banging on the door like my sister... the question is... what will they find?

As a witness to such a scene, I can assure you that whoever the person is and in whatever condition he may be found, it won't make much difference to those people who knows the person well. I can tell you that dead or alive, the fear factor, anger, insecurity, sadness, helplessness, a real mixture of negative feelings and reactions experienced by the relations in such conditions is overwhelming, to the extent of going overboard.

Dead or alive, the matter would be over within a few hours, but the ugly memories it leaves behind in the minds of all the affected would continue to haunt them for a long time to come.

In order to show that you care, and feel for them too, despite all your shortcomings, don't allow drugs to rob them of you. It's time to look into the mirror and see tomorrow is brighter than today. Let's become smarter and wiser than the evil that is seeking to claim our souls, by ravaging our physical body with drugs and alcohol.

If we do not become wise and make smarter decisions, then it will not be long before someone is standing over another open grave.

CHAPTER 2

# *You came from where?*

This may shock many but I was born and raised up in a Christian family. I am the fourth eldest son in a family of eight children. Like any other pure tribal Nagas, I'm also a Naga by birth and by blood. I come from a remote village-town in the hilly Indian state of Nagaland which is nestled among the finest natural reserve of north-east India.

We Naga's are mostly known by the outside world through our unique ethnic identity, rich cultural heritage and traditional values, passed on by our fore bearers from generation to generation.

Like many, my father prided himself in the rich heritage of our bloodline. You may be thinking, did his family come from royalty or a famous person? No! What I want you to realise is that every family line has a history of good or bad. For some families we love to sit our children down and tell heroic stories of family members, whether true or not. For other families we whisper to our children… hush… don't mention that name!

Whether we like it or not, you and I are writing history and someone is going to be mentioning our names and I wonder, is it going to be good or bad?

It is true we cannot make everyone speak good of us, but, it is preferred upon by human beings as their innate nature to be spoken well of by the majority rather than only a few.

If you don't agree, imagine someone speaking derogatory about the one you love… would you be happy?

Like many families, my Dad would sit us down around the fire on a winter's night and tell us of his bygone days. His face would glow with excitement as he narrated about his school days and later as a freedom fighter.

In school he studied with a competitive spirit, focusing on being a winner in life. He would tell many times, "Knowledge is books, and books is knowledge!" He treasured his school books that much, he would secretly carry his books away and hide them deep in the near forest where his parents would have sent him to collect firewood. In those days school books were to be treasured and Dad done just that.

At the end of his school days he passed with high grades, setting the stage that if he can do that, his children when they would arrive, could do the same, or even better.

Just after passing his 6th grade he was summoned by a Lieutenant General Kaito to join the Naga Revolutionaries in their fight for Naga's sovereignty. Thus, he got enlisted in 1956 and by 1961 he was made 2nd Lieutenant, and a year later was promoted to Captain. Having served for nearly 18 years as a Naga freedom fighter he joined, along with his comrades, the national India army. Later, having served for 20 years, he retired in the rank of Deputy Commandant.

I was born when my father was still working in the Border Security Force (B.S.F.) and it was not long before I realised that he was a very strict disciplinarian. His vision for his children was to instil the value of education and dignity of work in the minds of us.

He was always determined that none of his children, my six brothers and one sister who was the youngest, would be denied a chance for further education. To his credit, all of us could at least reach pre-university, but to my Dad's dismay, only a few of us would study further and graduate.

His dream of one of his children becoming somebody 'big' someday would undergo drastic change of direction very soon.

My Dad could not have picked a better mother than my Mum. My Mum was a very hard-working housewife, full of energy, arising with the dawn no matter how tiresome the last day had been. Together with Dad, they made a great pair and tried to get the best of everything for their children.

Dad would mostly stay away from home because his duty entailed guarding international borders between India and the surrounding countries… Pakistan, China, Bangladesh, and Myanmar. He would come home once or twice a year, but if he failed to come home he would still send money home regularly.

Mum on her part played the most timeless, back-breaking, major role in the family. We kept no domestic helper at home and the responsibility of taking care of all the children ultimately fell on her shoulders. She would wake up earlier than anyone in the colony to prepare breakfast, arrange water for wash-up, keep the school uniform ready for the younger lot; and when the kids woke she would make haste to send them to school on time.

After seeing off the children, she would prepare a meagre meal for herself and go to the field taking along the younger non school going kids. In order to support Dad, she would cultivate the water fields for paddy, and also do shifting cultivation for vegetables.

Those were hard times, with only one earning member in a family of 10 members and that was Dad. It became harder still when my three elder brothers got admission at the same time in different colleges far away from home.

My Mum found the new arrangement better because the younger kids didn't need much looking after, like years before, and with the free time and reserved energy she could put all her efforts into work, to support Dad who was finding it hard to pay the college fees.

Dad would often chastise her saying she should be working only at home, but Mum would keep on working both at home and in the fields, particularly when she realised that I also would be going to college very soon. Thus my 'Iron Lady' Mum continued sweating her fragile body out in the fields so that all her children could be given a proper education.

In spite of her hectic schedules, Mum tried her best not to neglect her spiritual life. She would attend church regularly and would also go to revival meetings. To her credit and love, I used to think that it is all because of her prayers that I am still alive today!

## *School days...*

For some people, it would seem that no matter what door they approach, it opens before them before they even knock. For others like myself, not only would the doors close in front of me, but they also appeared at times to be bolted and blocked up! In-fact, totally impregnable.

One door however that stayed open for me from my childhood was the fact that out of all my siblings, I was my father's favourite. I don't know why this was but I always had great favour with my Dad. Through all my faults and failures, this continued well until my pre-university years!

I was not always the sharpest pencil in the class as they say. I remember one day in particular when I was aged ten, I was sitting trying to solve a maths problem in class. I didn't know that my Dad was visiting the school that day and was in the adjacent room.

I stood up in class and I started to read a question aloud, "Find the value of...." However, I pronounced the word 'value' as 'valley.' Just as the words spilled out of my mouth, I heard this voice shouting, "STOP!"

I froze in terror, I knew that voice, it was my Dad commanding me to stop! I don't know if I was more shocked or embarrassed, but he entered the classroom I was in and I just became like a small child again. My bottom lip dropped, disappointing him again, I listened to what he had to say. He told me that I was wrong with my pronunciation and then taught me how the word 'value' should be pronounced. This trivial incident marked the wisdom of a sixth-class educated father.

It was a hard lesson to learn, being humiliated in front of my peers but through Mum's prayers and my Dad's incessant encouragement and discipline, I would improve.

Later that year I was ranked third in our class of 60 students. With having a coach like my Dad on my side, there was no going back. Receiving deserved appreciation and finding great joy in securing highest marks in exams, I made it my goal to beat all the other students in my class. I was very happy when I was given the *overall best student award* for two consecutive years.

I also proved my worth when I appeared (illegally) in both state H.S.L.C. and central C.B.S.E. (Class-X) Matric Examination in the same academic year, taking advantage of the difference in the exam schedule. I passed in 2nd and 1st class respectively (perhaps becoming the first student to kill two birds with one stone 'matrically!')

Soon after attaining my results, I collected all my necessary documents and Dad and I travelled to the only institute offering science courses – Science College Jotsoma. However, it was not plain sailing as I was denied admission. Even though I had secured more than the required marks in science and maths, they would not enrol me because they said I was too late!

Dad tried his best to move the Principal to reconsider my case but all attempts of coaxing and pleading turned futile. We went home feeling sad, but not with all hopes lost.

I had heard that the college had five seats reserved for those meritorious students passing out from the C.B.S.E. (Central Board of School Education).

I knew I still had a chance with a better C.B.S.E. result. Sure enough, I passed in first class and was eligible to apply (once again!) to become a science student.

I went alone this time and submitted the admission form with all the required documents. I was called to come in front of the Principal and he was surprised to see me. It was only across the hall that he had denied me a few weeks earlier.

Now here I was again, standing holding a file with all the necessary documents required to get admission in this premier institute. I studied him carefully as he took his time going through all my documents. Then sighing he said, "Everything is in order, you are accepted." At long last, I had become a science student!

## Debating and tribalism...

Socially and academically I was doing well by making new friends and then passing my first-year pre-university in first class. I also took interest in co-curricular activities. I had presented an own-scripted drama and a self-composed song in our college's freshers' day and in my second year was given the privilege to make a farewell speech during the parting social. It was then, I was to find out that debate was my forte. I took part in the college debate as a fresher and was later asked to represent our college in the state inter college debate competition at the State Academy Hall.

It was during my time at debate in college where I was about to have my first hands-on experience in 'tribalism.'

You might be thinking what has 'tribalism' got to do with drugs or alcohol? The dictionary states that 'tribalism' means...

> *"The state of existing as a tribe, or a very strong feeling of loyalty to your tribe."*
>
> *"A very strong feeling of loyalty to a political or social group, so that you support them whatever they do."*

Cambridge dictionary[6]

Whether we realise it or not, most of us have come from or still dwell in a 'tribalism mindset.'

A 'tribalism mindset' is when one becomes part of a group and no matter what the group does or seek to go towards, one follows.

This can be anything from a soccer, government, religion or to the extreme, a terrorist group. They all have one thing in common, whether right or wrong, they are bonded by a belief. They come together and so it is the same with an addict.

They have joined another tribe; learning the culture of that tribe, the language, the behaviour and before long, a representative, promoter of that tribe whether good or bad. They go from knowing little or nothing about the tribe to having the same habits, speech (which is normally slang or code), sickness and character traits.

Each year the college held an election for new executives and representatives with great enthusiasm and fanfare. The contesting candidates would go pleading even their juniors, begging for their votes. They would inform their parents who in turn would send money for their election expenditures. With money in your pocket there was no dread or shortage of voters and friends. Shops, restaurants, hotels in the college campus, that usually were deserted would be packed to capacity, all at the expense of the contesting candidates. Vehicles would be arranged to transport students coming from the town especially by those candidates contesting against strong opponents. Hostel to hostel, room to room campaigning, alliances among tribes, assessments and harassments... indeed, it was an exciting period when studies were given the back seat except by the 'book-worms.'

I was put under pressure to contest for the *class representative* seat by the Allied Tribes in a class of 120 students. Unfortunately, students from my tribe and the Allied Tribes formed only 35% of the total strength. My opponent would easily win with 65%.

I didn't lose hope, and instead started visiting my classmates, even those from my opponent's tribe, seeking their valuable votes.

Election day arrived and after a brief introduction and speeches by both the intending candidates, the presiding officer of the day scribbled on a big blackboard two names, my name and the name of my opponent.

The 107 voters who turned up were instructed to just write either 1 or 2 on the ballot paper and nothing else. I was number 1 and the other person was number 2. The voting began. Assessments charts were laid on the desks by both parties' *right hands* and with every vote cast, a cross or a tick was made. With the last voter having casted his vote, the counting began, I needed 54 votes. After the final counting, the presiding officer wrote on the black board.

Number 1 = 53

I sighed, "Ah no... But yeah, I had expected it." I felt sad thinking I'd lost, but not so much unhappy. At least it had been a tight and a close fought contest. The presiding officer continued in writing....

Number 2 = 51

For a moment in time I did not understand, as the figures were not coming together when he wrote...

Invalid votes = 3

I jumped from my seat, joining in the victory shouts with my dear friends, some of them carrying me on their backs singing 'hip, hip, hooray!' My opponent demanded a recount to which I obliged, but still the result remained the same – 53-1's, 51-2's and 3 invalids with large 0's.

I rang my Dad to tell him about the outcome and asked him for some money to host a small party for all my friends that had voted for me.

During that party, my friend Tim, told me what had taken place the night before the election. My opponent and myself had visited their hostel room and spoke to Tim and his roommate. We sat together and chatted away for a while and left them to decide what way they were going to vote.

After we left, Tim told his roommate that they should split their votes. He said that he would vote for my opponent, and so his friend should vote for me. His friend complied and voted for me but, Tim never did cast his vote for my opponent, and that starry night I hugged him and told him to leave science and pursue a career in politics! Tim laughed away at my suggestion and continued to pursue and complete his science degree and found a good job as a state government servant in the rank of an officer.

If it hadn't been for his quick thinking and those three invalid votes, I never would have had a seat as a class representative.

## *The representative...*

Life as a class representative was hectic but quite enjoyable too. I tried to dispense all my obligations in my best capacity. All these were to take a back seat when I got the opportunity to become a representative of a different kind.

Just over a month before my final pre-university exam, I was approached by our college general secretary and the literary, symposium and seminars secretary of the Naga Students Federation in my hostel room. I was asked to represent our state in the debate competition, in the 2nd north-east Youth Cultural Festival to be held shortly. My Dad taught me that in life when opportunities come, we must be able to grab them and I gladly grabbed the opportunity. I was off to the debate!

After a tiresome two days journey by road, we reached the capital. Throughout the journey I prepared for the debate and in my mind, I ran over all the points I had gathered with the help of our English professor, on the given topic, *'The youth are losing their cultural identity.'*

Just before the competition the following night, I learned that I was the youngest of all the participants, both in age and academically. I felt so nervous, particularly when I picked up my lot and found myself to be the first competitor to take the stage, and by virtue of being the first speaker, I was made the leader (of our group) in the opinion of the house. One of the three judges for the competition stood and after all formalities added that, each leader of the house would be given an extra three minutes after all the participants had taken their time.

When my name was announced, I stood and rattled off the well-rehearsed speech I had in my head, just going a few seconds over the allotted five minutes. After everyone had taken their time, I stood again and debated for three minutes with my *points of cancellation* which I had noted as my opponents had spoken.

As my time in the spotlight ended, I saw the judges gathering together and after a few minutes of hushed discussion, they were ready to declare their scores. As I stood waiting in anticipation for the decision, it was like time had stood still before the names were announced. The spokesperson approached the microphone. The time had come. I could hear my heart pounding in my chest.

He cleared his throat and began his announcement; number one position was… my name was not mentioned. Number two position was… still my name not mentioned. Number three position was… my happiness was becoming deflated, still no mention of my name. Number four position… Anato. Wow! I was so happy, I had made it!

Yet for some reading this book, you might be thinking, number four does not count, but it comes back to how we see things. We can look at something and become discouraged that we weren't picked as number one, two or three or we could take encouragement that number four is a lot better than number 10, 50 or 100. So many times, even as a follower of God, it can seem that God has forgotten about us, but He never forgets about you or me, it always comes back to our understanding of how we see things.

I don't know about you, but for many families that have more than one sibling, and when this is the case, their attitude is, if someone picks a fight with one of us, the others would be stepping in and saying, "Pick on him, you pick on all of us!"

One would think when a person would have 10 older brothers than oneself and a younger one, God help those who would pick on you. But not so, the Bible tells us of the 10 older brothers of Joseph, they did not defend him but actually sought to destroy him as found in Genesis 37.

Even with a God-given dream in the heart of Joseph one would think, it was onwards and upwards for Joseph, but not so, his life was about to go on a total downward spiral and he was not in control of it. His brothers waited for an opportune time and they stripped his father's coat off him, took him by force and dropped him into a pit, then sold him as a slave to Ishmaelite merchants. What is it like to go from being favourite to being unwanted?

Cast into a prison for at least two years, and they were not like the prison of our day. These would have been grim, dark, rat infested, in many instances the prisoner was chained to a wall. And yet it was in that season of darkness, where no one knew of his existence and it was impossible to get out of prison, the very thing that caused the start of the downward spiral was sharing a dream. His cell mates were now sharing dreams with him. The very thing that can take you on a downward spiral can be the very thing that if you turn it around, can cause you to help others and yourself.

Joseph interprets the dream of his cell mates, and the interpretation reaches Pharaoh's ears that a dream interpreter is under his care and... he's an accurate interpreter.

Pharaoh then has two dreams and guess who he sends for?

Joseph was brought forth from the cell, cleaned up and presented before the Pharaoh, where he shared the interpretation of the dreams and Pharaoh bearing witness that the interpretation was true, entrusted Joseph to the degree that he became his Vizier, second in command. Now that is power one would think. But for Joseph, he had something else that was more important to him than power over people. For Joseph it was relationship. He sought wholeness and wholeness is never complete when a piece is missing. Joseph sent for his family who thought he was dead.

When his family came to his home, he cried over them at the banquet in the realisation that it was God that had went before him, it was God that was the real restorer of his family. What the devil had planned to destroy him, God had turned around for good.

No matter what part of the path you are on, God has a plan for you and in His plan, it can only be good!

The night that I was at the debate, I didn't get the first position that I was longing for but God knew the position that I would attain well before the judge. Instead of us becoming hard-hearted, we must become a person of acceptance yet willing to change, willing to become better, willing to know that something greater is ahead. When it was announced position four, I was happy! For I know now, that what God starts in you, He is well able to finish, otherwise He would not have started.

I was happy to know that I had secured fourth place as per the judges' score card. My joy knew no bound when our team was declared overall winner of the contest.

*'There has never been the slightest doubt in my mind that the God who started this great work in you would keep at it and bring it to a flourishing finish on the very day Christ Jesus appears.'* Philippians 1:6 (NLT)

*'Is there anyone here who, planning to build a new house, doesn't first sit down and figure the cost so you'll know if you can complete it? If you only get the foundation laid and then run out of money, you're going to look pretty foolish. Everyone passing by will poke fun at you: 'He started something he couldn't finish.'* Luke 14:28-30 (NLT)

# CHAPTER 3
# *Life as a Medico...*

My pre-university days were ending and with the final examination approaching, I prepared my lesson with every part of my being. Completing the exam I went home and began the long 'wait and watch' period. When the results were declared, I collected the 'mark sheet' and found out that I had passed, by securing distinctions in chemistry, physics and biology.

With the results, I decided to pursue the M.B;B.S (Bachelor of Medicine; Bachelor of Surgery) course and soon after declaration of the results, I entered into Andhra Medical College, Visakhapatnam, Andhra Pradesh, India.

This was the first time I had ever travelled outside the area where I lived, and I found myself homesick. I was all alone in an entirely new environment of a large city blistering with mankind of different tradition, culture and religion. The college authority became my sole guardian and they had dispensed their first duty by allowing me to stay in the hostel even before my admission in the college.

Just as I was feeling lonely, then, destiny brought along a friend who was the total opposite of me. He hailed from a rich, affluent family; and I was from a middle-class background. He was fat and short; I thin and tall. He wore spectacles; I didn't! Despite our many differences, we gelled well under the circumstances and tried to bring out the best from what fate had brought together.

Soon we started going to classes together on his motorcycle and spent most of our time in each other's company, going to the beach, frequenting the city's hot-spots to explore, meeting and making new friends.

A month into college life, preparation for our *freshers' day* began in full swing. I was supposed to present a song but, during the last days of the rehearsals the professor-in-charge, instigated by my seniors, asked me to perform a different song. I said I couldn't as I did not know it. He persisted saying I could perform it. With only a few hours left to practice and perform, finally, I relented.

That same evening, I told one of my friends about my predicament, and ever so helpful, he went to a music store and bought a music album of the latest hit movie that had the song on it. We wrote the lyrics down and practised late into the night.

Freshers' day arrived and I took the stage towards the end of the programme. As I hit the chorus note of the song, the audience chimed in and started clapping in unison. I felt the thrill of being in the spotlight and was very happy. When I got a standing ovation, I was thrilled.

The next time I took to the stage, I had my electric guitar and belted out *'Wind of Change'* by the Scorpions. The crowd was not disappointed; afterwards they all gathered around to congratulate me.

Soon after, I jumped headlong into my studies and made it my motto to never miss even a single class, except under inevitable circumstances. I prepared well for my first semester examination but found a problem with the new question patterns and could not write the examination papers satisfactorily. Sure enough, I missed first class by just a few marks. I made it a point to first study and understand the question pattern for the coming semesters. I was rewarded well, when I passed my second semester in 1st Class, having secured distinction in one subject.

## *The great diversion...*

My journey down to the gates of hell and shame began one winter vacation when I did something so self-destructive, it would become my second repulsive nature for years to come.

My friend and I were on a train journey one night and the train had stopped mid-way at one of the large stations for the night. We were absolutely exhausted and our bodies were aching following a non-stop two-day journey on a crowded Indian train, if you know or can imagine what that is like?

I sought a chemist to relieve our stressed-out, aching condition, but when I found one, instead of asking for the usual medicine to relieve such a condition, I took the courage and requested the shopkeeper for an effective painkiller which is not given without a doctor's prescription. The chemist complied after my brief self-introduction and with some gentle persuasion. I bought the drug and hurried back to my room where my friend was waiting.

I was hoping this would relieve our symptoms, however, there was a certain degree of hesitation and fear in my mind of taking the drug since I knew that it was commonly abused. I also had heard of many cases of death following intake of such a drug. Still, we encouraged each other and took the drug beyond the recommended dose. We told our misguided selves that it was going to be a one-time experience, not realising that it was going to be one such experience that would open the door to an entirely different world. A world where I was going to destroy myself, my senses, and my career.

After 20-30 minutes of taking the drug, all tiredness, body aches and anxiety had disappeared. As we sat, we found ourselves more talkative, confident and energetic and smoked the night away, boosting our system with even more drugs to transport ourselves into a non-existent world of euphoria.

The next day, hours before we were to depart to our different destinations, we bought more of the same drugs for our journey even though it was illegal for us to possess or smuggle such kind of drugs. Not wanting to be caught by the police, I emptied a small container, cleansed it thoroughly, then made a plus (+) incision at its 'mouth' and patiently inserted the drug capsules, one by one, inside the belly of the emptied container.

On the second leg of my journey alone, I took out the stuffed container openly as it looked like a normal everyday usage container, went to the toilet, extracted the capsules and washed them down my system with water, and returned to my berth.

The drug induced 'high' was worth any risk, or ingenuity on my part. At least, that's what I thought in my devil-drilled mind.

## *The wolf in sheep's clothing…*

The drug habit stuck, and the mode of smuggling *the stuff* during vacations remained the same. When at home, I would pretend there were no such evil habits, nor would I give any indication that I was abusing drugs. At the nascent stage of my addiction, I would refrain from taking any drugs during my stay at home, and instead kept myself busy taking part in various social and even church activities. At the same time, I devoted two-three hours daily in studies.

On various occasions, ironically, I was given privilege to warn other youths on topics on drug abuse and alcoholism.

At that time the word 'abuse' had no meaning in my 'neo-habitual' dictionary. I thought that I could give it up anytime and in truth, I didn't have a guilty conscience.

One day, just before going back to my study place, I met another friend after a gap of many years. He was pursuing his B.A. degree and was home on vacation. He asked me to get a few vials of the drug from a medical shop by identifying myself.

We went to his residence and bolted ourselves in. Inside his bedroom, he took out a disposable syringe and filled it with one ampoule of drug. The other, he said was for me. I was asked to administer the drug intravenously (I.V.) as he started flexing his arm.

With my studies, I knew how, where and in which vein I had to give the injection but I refused to do it. Noting my reluctance, he calmly and assuredly said that it would be the last, and even advised that I should take it as a 'one time' experience.

With a weakening resolve and diminished will-power, I agreed and administered the drug slowly as he took another puff on his cigarette. When I was done injecting him, he sat motionless for a few minutes with glazed eyes, and then he took out another syringe and loaded it with the remaining ampoule of the drug and 'pushed' it into my system.

We sat listening to our music for a long time, watching the world we knew disappear like the vapour from our cigarettes. I never realised that night, I would never meet him again, he died shortly after that of a drug overdose.

## *You reap what you sow...*

Back in the college, I had been somebody to reckon with in those days and my pride liked it that way. Appreciated and admired by others for my brilliance and yet, no one knew about the habit, forming within me.

One morning I received a phone call from my Dad. He was checking up on me and wanted to know how I was doing with my studies, then he asked, "How is your health?"

Immediately, my character changed from the son who loved him, to a son who would deceive him. I assured him everything was alright. I went to hang up the phone and his voice spoke again… he asked, "Are you going to class?"

I replied an affirmative, "Yes, sure!"

Deception and lying was now becoming my best buddies but where would these new buddies lead me to?

A little later, a friend who was also studying medicine in a different medical college, paid a casual visit to our hostel. His family was from Saudi, were very wealthy, and he was not afraid to show it. He loved showing off the money and was always purchasing the latest 'thing' that was made available.

A new style motorbike had just been launched and of course he was front in the line to secure a model, but even purchasing the latest model was not good enough, he still had to get it modified further.

When he asked, "You want to go for a ride Anato?" Well, how could one say no? Instead of going to school like I told my Dad, I went for a ride on his bike.

I took off on the bike through the town showing off. I was enjoying the freedom of the bike on the street and just had approached a busy intersection at high speed. My eye caught an old man crossing over the road but he didn't see me coming towards him. Immediately, I blasted the horn but I never got his attention.

Getting ready for impact, I braked hard and swerved. Coming to an abrupt halt, the back of the bike spun around causing the back wheel to swipe the old man right off his feet. (Fortunately, as I learnt later, the old man suffered only some minor injuries, and was discharged after a few minutes of treating the bruises and scratches.)

As of me, I went flying into the air, some six metres, and my face crashed onto the hard road.

Blood started to gush out of my mouth and I felt something like a betel nut (supari) in my mouth. As I spat out the mixture, I realised that I'd knocked out my upper incisor tooth. It was much later that I learned, I had also chipped four other teeth, as well. I mumbled out two of my friend's names and my hostel's address to the gathering crowd and blacked out.

When I regained consciousness, I was lying on the hospital bed. The staff had I.V. drip lines into both of my arms. A cluster of friends, doctors and nurses stood anxiously around the bed.

When the X-rays and other investigation results returned, they revealed a fractured skull, a fractured nose, one lost incisor, four broken teeth, a lacerated upper lip that required three stitches and lots of bruises and blood loss.

Treatment and recovery would take nearly two months and I grimly realised that I wouldn't be able to sit my third semester exam that was just a month away.

It was during this time, under treatment in the orthopaedic ward of King George hospital, that I was confronted again with my nemesis of drug abuse. I was in the throes of pain, aggravated with anxiety and depression, when during one of my friend's visits they suggested that I take a drug, not prescribed by the doctor, to ease my pain. I thought it over, which was a grave mistake, and realising I had nothing to lose, told him to get the *stuff* which he brought promptly.

It was then I had a thought of making long-term decisions for my life and not short-term decisions, but for now, it was just that, only a thought! I excused my depraved mind with thoughts of not having to prepare for exams, not being a habitual user, being wrecked with physical pain and mental agony, and with a 'can give up' attitude, thus beginning that day of wrong judgement and perception, I started taking the drug along with other prescribed drugs, whenever I felt a twinge of pain hitting my body.

Even though I recovered outwardly, I could sense deep within, I had lost part of me physically, mentally and academically in that accident.

After losing out on my third semester exam, I started attending classes and began to study hard again. The character of drug abuse kept tormenting me quite often and I would succumb most of the time, by purchasing the drugs with my parent's hard-earned money as they continued to send the money for schooling fees and support.

Each time I would take the drugs, I would seek to convince myself by saying, "It will only be for a few days, then I'll give them up." Indeed, I would abstain from taking any for several days but the craving and lust was driving all peace out of my life and I would start abusing again. The days I would abstain, became lesser and lesser until complete addiction took hold.

The drugs were now doing damage and this young man who had such a sharp mind, was now struggling just to think. I had done everything I could to prepare and sit my exam, but what had been easy for me in many ways, was now such a struggle. My mind had been badly affected leading me to flunk in my last exam!

## *Lies and more lies...*

While my life was 'high' of euphoric damnation, precious academic years were lost without having made any progress in my career. Other than telling my parents about the accident, I never found the courage to tell them the truth or seek help, instead I'd simply answer when they asked, "Everything is great."

I became not only addicted to drugs but I had become an habitual liar. No matter who would ask, no matter where, if I could hide behind *everything is great* then I could survive for another moment. A never-ending vicious life of lies was the escape route that I took to protect myself from the harsh realities and to find myself in people's good books.

My life, then was filled with insecurities, fear, frustrations, guilty conscience and of course, lies! In order to counteract all these drug-induced complexities, I most ironically and devilishly sought the help of more drugs instead of God.

I remember one time I had returned home and my parents called me aside, they wanted to talk to me. Awkwardly, I was sensing something serious was about to happen. I was 23 years old then and I had never faced such a situation before. Behind the closed door they asked me the dreaded question… "Anato, are you taking drugs?"

I could feel the sweat breaking through my body quickly as I became embarrassed and ready to lie to the two people in the world that would have easily sacrificed their life for me, and in fact, many times had done.

I looked into my Mum's eyes and all I could see was love. Looking into my father's eyes, I could see dread, as if he was saying *have I raised you for this moment of time, to let us down?* I took a deep breath, smiled, and said, "No!"

Such relief came onto my parents faces. Yet behind my smile, my false mask of lying was now well fixed.

I never realised it at the time, but that moment was another turning point in my life. As if something snapped within me. The one who gave birth to me, the father who worked extra hours to provide for me… I stood before the two people in all the world who gave everything for me and I could not be honest with them.

Recovery from what I lost at that moment, if I ever could come back to this place again, I would love to seek. For now, all I cared for was the next fix and how to get out of this corner of questioning.

They responded to my answer with a smile and were relieved at my response. It would be a path that I would now live, lies after lies, hiding the real me.

## There's a cost with suicide...

Allow me to go into more detail on the story I shared with you at the start.

One day, while I was at my parents' home, with my parents and sister, I slipped away from our common room, as I found myself uncomfortable in their company because I was still abusing drugs secretly. My mind was full of all the failures that had taken place in my life. One after another the images came, like a lion sensing the kill.

I saw myself, the people I had let down, exams that I could have passed but did not due to the now dullness of my mind, times I should have been somewhere that would have changed my life for the better but failed to turn up, and times I should have spent judiciously and sincerely studying, investing into my future instead of foolishly spending it on the fleeting pleasure of the present, with drugs.

As I allowed those images of a wasted life to take hold - images of hurt, despair, remorse, self-betrayal, wretchedness, condemnation, disappointments, failures, hopelessness... I found the gallery of my life filled only with the images of the worst possible things a person could ever have in a nightmare.

I locked myself inside my bedroom. Yet, it's interesting when I look back at how quick those images sought to paint a picture of a failed life. At no point did it remind me of those who loved me.

I remember very clearly thinking that, if I took my own life, then my family members would not suffer any more by my abusive nature. Instead of me concluding, *what is worse than having a son or daughter that is addicted... a son or daughter who was addicted and then died;* for then there is no more hope for the family.

I reasoned stupidly, that it was meaningless for me to remain alive if I could call it that. I decided to put an end to it all.

I took out the self-styled rope that was made from a bed sheet. I had split it into long pieces and tightly-rolled two pieces each, the ends I knotted to form one stout rope.

I then stood on my bed and tied it on the wooden beam on the roof, leaving just a sufficient length to make a noose that would grip my neck in its dead hold. This would keep my body hanging a couple of feet off the floor.

I took the other end of the rope and placed my head inside the noose and slowly started to tighten it around my neck.

It's a very dark place when you are in this situation. It's the place where you believe you are totally alone and no one understands why you are like this.

Out of nowhere, I began to sob uncontrollably in a sudden burst of emotion. My sister rushed to the bedroom door and started banging it.

At that moment when she was banging the door and calling my name, I was standing on the bed ready to take that final step of my journey in this world.

She called out my name again and again; but I didn't respond. I remained silent for a time then loosened the noose and also the other end of the rope and hid it. I was wiping the tears from my face when she forced the door open.

Later when I fell asleep, I wakened suddenly to find my sister standing watching over me. She had stayed with me the whole night, filled with remorse and anxiety.

I am sad to write this but the truth is, even after that, seeing my sister and my parents, it still had no effect on me. I would try suicide with a knife, rat poison, etc. Anything to escape this drug-crazed mind.

## *Evil unmasked…*

After a month, staying at home and just a few days before I left for college, I would attend Sunday devotional in our local Baptist church and ponder deep on what I was going to do with my life.

That evening the church leaders were invited back to our home by my parents to pray for me. They wanted to pray and bless me for my return to college, however, they were in for a surprise when, I opened up to them.

On being asked by the pastor if I had anything to say, I stood and with downcast eyes, I told the gathering that I was not what they perceived me to be.

For the first time, I was being honest with myself. I revealed my true identity… the drug abuser who was deceiving everyone including his own family.

I had been living a 'double personality' life, much to their shock and great sadness. My parents were totally overwhelmed. My mother cried sore as my father held her.

As my father did so, he looked at me. Disappointment and hurt were in his eyes. I could feel the pain and deep-seated agony eating away into his hope and peace. His eyes betrayed his usual calm and confident composure as disbelief clouded his mind and unspeakable sadness spread over his heart.

I wished he could cry his heart out like Mum who was still crying, and maybe, find some relief through the tears shed, but Dad seldom cried.

For those who were present in the room, there was no doubt, they were struggling to take in what they were hearing. For my parents, it was a bitter realisation and confirmation of their doubts, but even though it was hard for them to swallow my confession, they felt relieved to know that I was finally out with the truth.

The mountain that they thought they were going to be praying against to help me, stood even greater before them, but I thank God, it is not the size of the mountain that matters, it is the size of our God!

Time seemed to stand still, as they all stood and prayed to God, invoking His mercy, grace and forgiveness for me, while I knelt and pleaded to the good Lord to forgive me.

## *Just one more...*

After that night, I started trying to pick up the thread of my unfinished task and surge ahead again in my medical studies, but all the time I was fighting a losing battle with the insomnia taking hold. My normal biological sleep-wake cycle had been grossly affected due to constant drug abuse without any sense of time.

Normal sleep eluded me, even after taking sleeping pills. I could sleep only after taking high doses of sleeping tablets in addition to four or five capsules of drugs.

To think of those acute insomniac periods of my life today, as I go to sleep peacefully without taking any pills or drugs, I wonder if at all, was that really me?

With my system fully pumped up with abusive substances, still deprived of sleep even though my exhausted body was crying out to be rested, I would stay up late into the night even under the influence of sleep-inducing drugs along with other drugs or alcohol. I was on drifting into a deep sleep just as other hostellers were waking up.

By the time I woke up it would be too late to go to college. No wonder I missed so many classes and fell short in my exams.

Quite early into my life I started suffering from episodes of depression due to my drug habit. This behaviour of depression was of a different nature, because I would start getting depressed even when I was under the influence of the drugs which I usually abused, and as a drug addict I knew that shouldn't be happening.

It was within the range of normal for me to feel depressed for having betrayed my parents and spending their 'sweat-money' to feed my drug habit. Being irresponsible in my studies, living a life of lies, fooling my dear ones and my friends back home... I had many reasons to feel depressed in my sobriety. In order to get relieved, I would take drugs, that was the usual method I used to counteract it.

What could I do if I was attacked by depression even when I was high on drugs? I read deep into my pharmacology textbook and found one drug which I believed to be the best for my problem. Soon after, I started abusing my newly-discovered anti-depression drug whenever I got depressed, even while under the effect of my usual drugs of abuse.

Looking back, I realise I should have known better; the anti-depressant I discovered and abused, indeed brought relief, but only temporarily. I found myself in an even more complex situation from which I had no option other than to take the drug in a vicious cycle of addiction.

Did I know then, that there exists the best of any other options - God? I doubt it, because my drug-influenced mind never had enough sense of truth in it to take God, or even my life seriously.

From the day I first failed in my exam and realised that all my classmates would be moving on ahead in their academic career leaving me behind, I developed *inferiority complexity syndrome.*

I started thinking that I could not be counted as an equal among peers anymore; that even my juniors would start calling me a failure; that I won't be able to stand or speak boldly even among friends; that all who know about my failure would talk and laugh behind me. My addictive nature sought the help of drugs in order to build my confidence, or lose myself in my own world and forget about others.

The drugs helped me forget about my complexity problem and also boosted my confidence, but only so long as their effect lasted, while the real problem of inferiority complex remained.

My body had grown weak and I couldn't do any significant physical work, least of all any work that required physical exertions and stress. I was suffering from long-term adverse effects of prolonged drug abuse. My body would fatigue easily and quickly.

The adverse effects had also damaged my central nervous system, in particular, my brain. I could not think clearly, nor was I able to reason normally. My mind would get cloudy and exhausted as if it was in short supply of oxygen. I was unable to carry out even small works without stressing out my body and mind quickly.

In order to counteract the adverse effects, I would increase my drug intake and lose myself in my own created world of imagined peace and temporary relief.

Due to those conditions I would keep myself, most of the time, in my hostel room after class and tried to keep distance from the person who introduced me to the drug world.

Sometimes he would still call into my room and would invite me out. For old time sake, I went along. He would often visit me late in the night, fling a strip or half of a drug from the doorway, saying it was a 'present' and then leave.

Usually, when I did the drugs, I used to get my own 'stock' of them, but this time round, he started offering them to me freely.

It's interesting that when one is seeking to walk away from something, the very people who never would have given a person anything is now nearly begging for you to take it.

I accepted his 'gifts' but never used them. After a few days, I had accumulated enough of his 'gifts' to last me several days and would have cost me a large sum of money, had I purchased them on my own. I disposed of them all and remained 'clean' and sober for three to four months.

Then one day, with a new batch of students for their freshers' night, I was supposed to perform on stage, I went back against my word and took a few capsules and a tablet in order to boost up my confidence. I said to myself, 'just this one time.'

With the effect of the drugs running high, I took to the stage and performed a song. Being transported to the world of drug-induced fantasy, I never knew how the audience really felt about my performance.

That 'just once' habit stuck and I was back to square one and this time the habit had become stronger.

# CHAPTER 4

# *Passport embarrassment...*

My drug intake routine had spiralled out of control. The dosage increased and the side effects were imminent in the form of decreased appetite, loss of normal sleep, decreased activity and deteriorating 'skin and bone' health. Disrespecting my fragile health and dishonouring my commitment to my parents, I even started 'fixing' (injecting drugs) when I didn't get that same feeling of euphoria through oral intake. It helped when I became desperate to have immediate, desired effect of the drugs and thus, while my career remained stagnant, without making any progress, I graduated from 'popping' (taking drugs orally) to 'pushing/gunning' (same as fixing/ intravenously).

While I was in this state of completely deteriorated health, the college authority issued a notification requiring all the students of my batch to fill out our application form for the approaching examination and submit it at the college office. As usual they required a passport-sized photo to be attached along with the application form. I collected the given form and filled in the necessary details, then I searched for my passport-sized photo to be attached and attested as required.

When I couldn't find it, I decided to have a new photo taken. I washed up, put on a fresh formal shirt and headed for a professional photographer's outlet. The photographer was alone, I told him what I needed. He ushered me inside his studio and asked if I would like to fix my hair and face before taking the picture, pointing to a mirror and a basket that contained combs, face powder, cotton roll, water-spray bottle... I thanked him and looked at myself in the mirror.

I had long forgotten the last time I sought the service of any mirror; my drug nature had no interest in my outlook or general appearance. As I looked in the mirror, I beheld a face that looked quite different from the image I had carried of it - an emaciated face with prominent cheek bones and eye sockets covered only by skin that looked pale and quite unhealthy. As I looked, I imagined my skeletal-self among those abused and starving Jews in the concentration camps during World War II and realised sadly, that there was no difference between them and my present health status.

I could only see a pair of drug-burned, glazed eyes in the hollows. I felt so ashamed that I rolled out two cotton balls and made pads out of them, then inserted them one by one through my mouth, one each on the inside of my cheeks, to puff my face up and look at least presentable, albeit to a miniscule extent. When I was satisfied I sprayed water on my hair and combed it. All set, I called the photographer and asked him to take his best shot.

When it was done, I went to the washroom, removed the saliva-soaked cotton pads and deposited them in the dust bin and returned to the payment counter. The photographer was smiling but I knew it was not a normal kind of smile, therefore I didn't smile back.

I paid him and took the developed copies, stapled one of the newly taken photos to my application form and submitted it at our college office.

Then unlike other days when I would roam the city, or the beach in leisure after my work/class was over, I rushed to my hostel room haunted by the image I saw of my face in the mirror at the studio. Shame gripped my heart and my mind to such an extent that I didn't have the guts to show my acutely starved face to anyone. I stayed indoors for more than an hour, then reality dawned on me that others had captured my face in its present form long ago, if I was to die then and there, that is the image they would remember of me.

That realisation crushed my spirit to the core, and in order to overcome my miserable state of health and mind I took a generous quantity of drugs, waited for the effect to work in my system, then after nearly two hours of staying inside behind my bolted door, I released myself and went to the beach with the temporary confidence I derived from the drugs.

I would never know how I got back to my hostel that night, for I'd remember only the first few hazy setting hours after I had bolted out from my room, going to the beach, desiring to plunge into the sea and be no more.

## *Doctor! Doctor!..*

My drug addiction had already taken a heavy toll on my health. I became disease-prone and my immune system had weakened, and this was proved one night when I found myself unable to walk normally, due to acute pain in my left leg. I took some prescription drugs but the pain still persisted.

The next morning, I noticed a painful swelling in my groin and I found it even more difficult to move about. I knew that it was an absccss formation (collection of pus) and tried to cure myself.

I took some antibiotics and painkillers, then plunged a syringe needle into the heart of the abscess to extract the pus. Even after several attempts, I could not drain thc pus. It was only later, when I applied pressure with both hands and clenching my teeth, I squeezed out 250-300ml of pus and felt relief for the first time in three agonising days.

I went to the hospital and was admitted by a doctor to the students' sick ward and found myself to be the only patient.

One lonely afternoon, while I was sleeping post-lunch period, my left femoral blood vessels (main blood supplier of legs) ruptured. I woke up when I felt some warm sticky liquid on my bed and to my utter shock found myself in a pool of blood - the precious blood still spurting out from my eroded blood vessels. I tried to gauge the blood flow with a towel but to no avail. The towel was soaked wet and the blood kept oozing out. I shouted, in despair, at the top my voice, "Sister, sister! Doctor, doctor..."

While pinching myself to remain conscious and at the same time pleading to God, "Not now, not here, oh Lord, please... I don't want to die lying in a sick bed all alone and so far away from home."

Soon a nurse came rushing along with a lady doctor trailing closely behind, but they rushed back and returned with the head of the cardiology department and other doctors and nurses.

They cut through my blood-soaked clothes and the head himself tried to stop the blood flow by applying pressure bandage while giving out orders. The nurses rushed about fixing me with bolus N/S (normal saline) and transfusing blood in order to raise my blood pressure and stabilise me.

After checking all my vital signs, the head ordered that I be shifted to the acute surgical care unit ward. Just before seeing me off in a wheelchair, he turned to me and said, "Mr. Swu, if you had slept for another few minutes then you would have died of haemorrhagic shock." (Death due to massive blood loss).

I had lost around two litres of blood! As I was pushed to the two-bedded room of the A.S.C.U., I thanked God for still keeping me alive and conscious.

## *The surprise visitor...*

One afternoon, while taking rest in the A.S.C.U. ward, I heard a knock on my door and as I said, "Enter!" Behold, there stood my Dad escorted by one of my younger friends, Mr. Jamir. He was another nominee from my area who, unlike me, was studiously pursuing medicine in the same college. Taking note of my critical condition, he had dutifully informed my parents.

Dad travelled alone all the way from our home town. Spending the family's precious resources for one of his sons who, once 'an apple in his eye' had become the 'black sheep of the family.' Sorrow, sadness and deep concern were written large on his aged face, even though he tried to mask them. He asked how I was, to which I mumbled, "Getting better."

He said a thanksgiving prayer to God for his safe journey and for the opportunity to visit me. As he prayed, I cursed myself for putting such a heavy burden on his old, weary shoulders. He said nothing for a few minutes and I knew he was sad, actually, very sad indeed.

During those 24 days in the hospital after his arrival, the only thing that Dad was happy about was me eating well. He encouraged me to eat as much as I could since my diet was unrestricted. Knowing that I secretly smoked, he lectured on how smoking decreases our appetite and spoils our health. True to his words, as I abstained from smoking, my appetite increased and I began to gobble up almost everything he brought for me.

My health improved dramatically after Dad's arrival, and I was discharged pending review of my health status after a month. No sooner was I discharged, and even before we had booked our tickets to go home, Dad told me that his biggest fear during his time with me, was to return home with the tragic news of my demise to Mum. I realised what he meant and bowed my head to his words, in shame.

## *A recluse...*

Before we reached home, the local gossip had spread about my hospitalisation. Like 'Chinese whispers' the truth of a statement becomes distorted as people pass it from pillar to post, even for some, adding their own little spin to it.

Some people were even saying that I had become handicapped. Indeed, I was still unable to walk normally and had developed limping on my left leg and therefore I was reluctant to go home for fear of being marked as handicapped or an outcast.

Reaching our home town, I felt so embarrassed, for the first time in my life, to walk along the streets where I'd once walked and played happily with my friends. The alleys that had once moulded my life had become strangers to me.

My social life became non-existent, as I seldom ventured out and even stopped going to the church. The urge to take drugs and escape from all harsh realities of my pitiable life and shattered ambition kept hitting me hard.

My health had still not fully recovered as expected. I'd just limp around inside the house, finding with great difficulty to even climb stairs, never mind doing any work of significance.

Then one day a doctor relative suggested I go for an M.R.I. (Magnetic Resonance Imaging). He referred me to one of his colleagues at a different hospital out of our state. I met the referred doctor, a neurologist who carried out all the necessary investigation at a concessional rate. He told me that I had lost the power of my quadriceps (main muscle of the leg) and doubted if I would ever get back to normal.

The news broke my heart that much, that when I returned home, I lied to my parents telling them that I would recover soon. My lifeboat was rocking hard in this spiral of devastation after devastation. The years I had sown drug abuse into my life, was now claiming its harvest.

I gradually started constructing an invisible wall around me. Not only would this keep people out but what I did not realise, it would become another bondage in my life.

During this sad juncture of my tarnished life, one of my aunts advised that I go to a prayer and healing centre. She had told me that she'd been there herself with a constant pain and bleeding from her womb. After prayer and fasting she was healed completely. What the doctors and medicines couldn't cure during her two to three years of suffering was just healed within a few days through fasting and prayer.

In hearing this and knowing she was an honest person and would never make such a story up, I pondered over her suggestion. I realised that there was no harm in finding out about this spiritual form of healing, even though it was in contradiction to what I, relied on medically and preferred upon in those days.

# CHAPTER 5
# *A place of miracles...*

It was decided that Mum would go along with me to this humble place of miracles. I was more or less going there as a tourist who was more interested in knowing what this 'cure without doctors and medicines' was all about.

Thus, with a flickering faith, if I had any, and after a tiresome journey, Mum and I reached the prayer and healing centre in Ayinato, and I was taken aback in my thinking when I saw it. It had no telephone or television or newspaper or shop of any kind.

To attain basic commodities, we would either have to walk a long distance or take the bus to locate the nearest shop.

During the scheduled services the Pastor did most of the preaching. Along with him was a woman leader, a warden and 10-12 prayer warriors.

Another interesting figure was the chaplain. When he would visit us, he would talk about his past life and how he came to be a chaplain. In finding his testimony worth mentioning, I have taken the freedom to trail off my story to write his, based on what he narrated to me.

## *A testimony within a testimony...*

Lt. Shikhu Swu was of short stature, bulky and a bespectacled man with a charming persona. He and my father had served together as Naga revolutionaries under FGN during their mid-20's.

Unfortunately, he was captured by the Indian Army and was sentenced to three months imprisonment, but he would still be in prison for many more years even after the stipulated term.

During his stay at Malwai Special Jail in Shillong, Meghalaya, many preachers came and proclaimed the Gospel to the inmates, but nothing could move or change their stony hearts.

Then one day, one of God's chosen visited them and said that they were detained neither by the Govt. of India nor by the State Govt. of Nagaland, but their sins were the cause behind their extended sufferings, and if they repent and confess their sins, God would release them. And if they would not, then they would die in the jail and won't be able to see their loved ones again.

Their life could be freed, and God had sent a warning to them that He, being the same God of Abraham, Isaac and Jacob, the One who saved Daniel from the lions' den and the same One who saved Shadrach, Meshach and Abednego from the blazing flames of fire – could do it for them.

Until that day, Lt. Shikhu had never learned to forgive or be forgiven. The spirit of vengeance always stoked the fire of hatred within him and avenging his unjustified and extended detention had become the main goal of his survival.

During his days as a Naga insurgent, he was serving as a P.S to the N.S.C.N. (IM) leader, Issac Chishi Swu, but his capture and subsequent incarceration had put an abrupt halt to his Naga political career.

He felt utter contempt for the Indians and hatred had made him blind spiritually, but with the arrival of the God's chosen and the warning that he could change direction in his life, his mind set changed and he began confessing his sins. Soon the grace and power of the Lord started working in his life. He began to see the brighter side of life and started giving thanks to God.

Then after having served seven years of illegal imprisonment, he was freed. By then he had lost around 30kgs and had contracted several health problems.

Despite all his hardships and untold persecutions, Lt. Shikhu had finally learned to forgive and even before his release he had all but forgotten about his revenge. Instead, he committed his life to Jesus Christ and became one of his witnesses.

He, along with like-minded friends in Christ, started to go from village to village spreading the Good News, and as the Holy Spirit began to work among them, many people accepted Christ as their Saviour and received blessings through them.

Not long after Lt. Shikhu received his calling as a chaplain at the prayer and healing centre. He dedicated his life to serve the spiritual needs of others with a smile that made it easier for any laymen or visitors to narrate their problems without any reluctance and get counselled and comforted. (It was then I met him.)

*- (Written as told - by permission.)*

# The fast...

Shortly after Mum and I got accustomed to the ways and practices of the centre and their great thirst for knowing God, we were allocated 30 days to fast and pray. During that period, we would not eat food, just drink water and stay in prayer. I realised that even though I'd come to the centre for my leg problem, it was of secondary nature and concern.

The primary and utmost importance was my spiritual health. It transpired that, if I could re-organise my life as God directed and dedicate my entire being to Him, then ultimately my physical problem and other associated shortcomings would be taken care of by the good Lord; but being a person of little or no faith, it was a very hard thing for me to do.

Mum, on her part prayed and fasted with all her body, mind and soul, and it was mostly because of me that she placed herself as a bargaining chip in the mighty court of God. She would often wake up in the middle of the night and pray while I slept soundly, and it was credit to her unwavering faith that, towards the end of the fast, I found improvement in my health. My limping had diminished and I could almost walk with a normal gait.

At the end of the fast, the pastor, the chaplain and the prayer warriors congregated in our room and after an inspiring and encouraging talk, they prayed for us in all earnest.

As we were praying, one of them whispered in my ear that if I went back to my old habit of drug abuse, I would not be able to revisit the centre. I was to remain vigilant and strong at all times.

Saying; 'Amen,' Mum and I stood from where we knelt and shook hands with all of them.

They said, in parting, that we were blessed to have come to the centre and that I'd be of great blessing in the lives of other people too, if I didn't stray off the right path, and follow God's commandments.

Bidding 'adieu' to all, Mum and I left for our home sweet home.


## *A spiritual family...*

After the prayer centre, I was soon back in the college with renewed ambition. I tried to leave all my past behind and pursue my degree with all that I could give. I started attending the classes regularly and concentrated deeply in my studies.

Once while studying, I was visited by a missionary and his companion in my hostel room. They introduced themselves as members of a Christian community and were active in over 90 countries, committed to sharing the message of God's love with others.

The missionary had been an engineer with a lucrative job, but after receiving the call to proclaim the Gospel, he left his job and started preaching about God.

Soon, he took it as his mission to spread the Word of God to the deaf-mute communities and even founded a small church especially for them.

They prayed for me and invited me and my friend to their church. The following Sunday we went along and we were received warmly by the missionary and around 30-40 handicapped people. Once inside, we were introduced to the congregation through sign language by the missionary. The programme highlights were - choreography by the mute and a skit about the Good Samaritan by the deaf-mute. A short sermon followed and finally the service concluded with a prayer.

Throughout the programme I stood in awe and shame in my innermost being to realise how my soul was handicapped while those of the deaf-mute were full of health and filled with peace.

Through this missionary, I came across another missionary couple from Australia and their family who were supervising the international work in a larger town. Jonathan and his wife Sue (uncle Jon and aunt Faith as they were called) started visiting me in my hostel room and began to teach me about the love of God. They often invited me over to their residence and even encouraged to call on them whenever I needed help of any kind. I started visiting them whenever I was free.

During our meetings I was privileged to be taught the salient features and etiquettes of a true believer, and the doctrines and principles of the Holy Bible. I was given assignments and Bible study by uncle Jon who would encourage me to memorise the Scriptures. He would always send me back to my hostel with Biblical tracts and other related materials for me to read. Some days, we would just listen to Christian music or watch Bible documentaries.

After almost two years, the time arrived for them to go back to Australia. On the day of their departure, they came to visit me for the last time, but sadly, I was attending class and by the time I returned they'd already left, leaving a small note that said "Jesus loves me and they love me too" and that, "I would be missed."

I made haste to the train station, as I happened to know how they would be travelling through the note they'd left. By the time I reached the station, their train was already on the platform and, even though I knew their train number and train name, with the amount of carriages on the train, I didn't know where they were.

With an utmost desire to see them off, I told the station manager of my dilemma. He phoned the station announcer and they announced a person by my name waiting at the counter, desiring to meet an Australian family leaving on the train, but when they didn't turn up, I requested if I could make the announcement.

I took the microphone and announced with a loud voice, "Your kind attention please. Uncle Jon and aunty Faith, this is Mr. Swu. If you are hearing this announcement, please come over to the station kiosk." I repeated thrice and waited anxiously.

Just as the announcement for their train's departure in a short while was being made, I saw uncle Jon running towards the kiosk.

I ran towards him and while shaking his hands he threw his arms around me and held onto me. We ended up talking for a while and went together to their carriage. There I met aunt Faith who was seated along with the children. Filled with emotion, we chatted as if we had not seen each other for a long time.

Then the train's final whistle sounded and we stood and embraced each other for the last time. I disembarked onto the platform and stood all alone, waving and watching them wave back.

As the last bogie of the train faded from my sight, it left me with only the memories of those loving people who it had carried away to a faraway country.

That was the last time I saw them, but not the last time I would hear about them. Uncle Jon kept in touch through email and inland posts, sometimes sending books and other materials relating to the teachings of the Bible.

I praise and thank the Lord for all the love, care and kindness shown to me through the blessed life of uncle Jon and his family.

It would be unfair and a big lie if I deny the fact that I abused drugs on occasion during my association with them. I had told them of my past and they knew that I would be under the influence of drugs sometimes when they came to meet me. Despite my abusive nature, they never gave up on me and even had the heart to keep in touch through correspondence, long after they'd left.

## Amid dark forces...

My life as a medical student dragged on somehow with innumerable excuses via accidents, ill-heath etc. I was in my final year but I still could never give up drugs completely. Every time I felt myself sinking deep in the quagmire of depression, sleeplessness or loneliness, I sought drugs, the cause of all such emotional and physical problems in order to find relief and temporary solutions.

It was a situation that betrayed logic, due to the change in the normal functioning of the brain because of drugs. I would start to take drugs for days or weeks together, then stop abruptly for some time, till I again found myself in the same situation that had propelled me to abuse them.

This 'cycle' seemed never-ending and I found myself in a giant 'whirlpool of deadly consequences' from which I found no strength or way to get out.

Gradually I'd made it a habit to indulge in drugs for as long as I desired, then just weeks before my exam I'd control myself and abstain from taking any as I prepared for examination, but with my drug supplier 'friend,' who was in the same hostel, it was very hard to commit myself even for those few weeks.

Knowing my financial disposition and having studied my nature thoroughly, he was still strolling into my room to offer me drugs on a daily basis.

One night before my exam, he walked into my room, and when he saw me studying he said nothing and stood looking around leisurely, for a while. Then out of the blue, he placed a bottle (half-empty) of a certain type of abusive medicine and few capsules of the drug I used to abuse and left my room. I was studying and thought for a while. I could take the drugs and crash-study for longer periods even covering more lessons, but I already knew the consequence of studying under the influence of drugs. I had, in my recent past, studied for hours together after taking drugs, covering many chapters at a time, but, during exam I would forget most of what I had studied, and so, that night I closed my eyes and asked God to help me overcome the temptation.

I did overcome the seen and unseen power of the adversary, but not for long; for soon after my exam, I returned to my room and took the drugs.

My life took a devastating turn when I came across one girl, let me call her *Miss Pretty*, for she was just that. She was slim, smart and very attractive. *Miss Pretty* was doing her Bachelor of Theology (B.Th.) in the same city. She was staying all alone in a rented flat near our hostel.

On learning that there were some students from her home area in the hostel, she paid a visit one afternoon and soon after we became friends. I found her to be a well-dressed, well-mannered and intelligent girl from a rich family background.

After a few days, I learned that she had passed her first B.Th. exam with 1st Class, but was on probation, having received stern warning from the college authority for her drug abuse, and that, she had already been expelled from the hostel where she had stayed with other student friends.

She introduced me to several other students who were sailing in the same boat of substance abuse. And worse than a fool guided by fools, I started to hang out with them, taking drugs, going for rides on the beach road, or watching movies in the city's big theatres, often freely as she would know the proprietors. Our sole objective was to procure drugs at all cost, get 'high' and escape the grim realities of life.

It is not my intention to belittle or demean anyone but, through *Miss Pretty* I came across many students from various theological institutes who were pursuing their career as theologians, far away from their families, and were abusing drugs or getting involved in illicit love affairs at the same time. Sadly, there are still many others who, once away from the protective and watchful eyes of their parents, become entrapped.

As with everything in life when it's a drug-themed relationship, *Miss Pretty's* relationship with me ended, and we lost contact.

## *Modern-day Samaritans...*

Again, my life was like a shipwreck. It was truly messed up. I had become a social misfit, not having a circle of friends that I could call my own or nowhere to fit in except for, with the druggies.

I became a loner, keeping mostly to myself with an ignorant perception of hope and faith. Every day I was being consumed by anger, fear, grief and despair over the thought of having destroyed my talented life and betraying all my loved ones.

Finding myself a stranger in the hostel, once full of friends and students wanting to be friends in my bygone years, I left the hostel and found for myself a small apartment not far away from our college.

It was during this lonely, sad phase of my life that destiny brought me under the wings of missionaries from another denomination.

These missionaries came to my apartment and that initial visit, became many as they tried their best to make me understand the principles on which their belief was founded upon. Every meeting ended in prayers and an invitation to their church which was held in a rented apartment. After months of meetings and discourses I started attending.

Soon, it became my bounden duty to accompany these missionaries in their mission. Aside from teaching me their ways, I thought I was called to 'drag along' because I could understand the local culture more so. Usually after class, two to three times a week, the missionaries would pick me up at an appointed time and together we would go about the city, seeking those who might believe in their faith.

Just as my pre-final exam approached, I became sick, consequent to my drug abuse. On consultation, I was advised to undergo surgery (skin grafting) for an ulcer on my right leg that had not healed and was becoming infected.

I had, by then fallen out of good terms with most of my good friends because of my addictive nature. As my family was living too far away from where I was now located, I had no one to call upon in the entire city to look after me in the event of my surgery.

Saddened and perplexed, I told the concerned doctor of my predicament. He told me that, being a medical student, the hospital will bear the expenses for surgery and medicines. All that was required was someone who could give consent for the operation and be there to take care of my needs after the surgery.

I could get someone who would write consent on my behalf for the operation, but I could think of no one who would spend their time and money to look after me post-op.

Thus isolated and resourceless, I was left on my own to ponder on what to do, when I received help from an unexpected source. The missionaries who had visited me months earlier learned of my problem and had entrusted a senior member to take care of everything. They had even found a lady caretaker who would be there to look after me till I recovered. Even though the journey with this church was for only a short time, something that I have always noted was just how well they looked after me in my time of need. Now isn't that something that we can all learn from?

Taking in the grace of God, I underwent surgery after the senior member signed the consent. Post-op, the caretaker looked after my needs and was with me from morning till evening, after which she left to spend the night at her house. The senior member would visit me three times a day bringing breakfast, meals and fresh clothes. I was visited by other church members and missionaries who prayed for my fast recovery and also cracked jokes to lift my spirit.

After 10 days, I was discharged and I made preparation to go home. I had informed my parents about the church and had asked them to send only the money and not to worry since I was being taken care of very well.

# CHAPTER 6

## *Nearly an amputee...*

When I arrived home, I was weak in health and mind. Having lost weight and being tormented by a constant thought of losing my dignity and honour to addiction, I was now clean and sober even though, the consequences of having abused drugs for such a long time were clearly visible through my deficient health.

I reached home along with my sister and youngest brother as we had planned to spend Christmas together with our parents, but just a day after I got home I was bedridden with high fever and pain in my left leg.

When the pain became too unbearable, I took some self-medication, even injecting myself with pain killers. My condition worsened and it became too difficult and painful to even move around casually. My leg had become swollen and blisters started to appear and puncture themselves.

On 21st December, just three days after reaching home, I was admitted back into hospital.

The doctor in the Emergency Room said that it would be better and less of a burden to our family if they amputate (cut off) my leg. I also wouldn't have to suffer for long duration as I would be discharged within a few weeks. However, one of the senior surgeons, on learning that I was a medico, said that they would try to save my leg depending on the X-ray results. He further added that, even if they carried out the operation as an option to amputation, I had only 50-50 chance of keeping my left leg.

Fortunately, my tibia and fibula (leg bones) were not infected, and soon after my admission, I was operated on. Then the agonising wait began for new healthy, granulation tissues to form and replace all the dead, necrotised tissues that had been removed during the first operation. Most of my left calf muscle was found to be infected and thus had been removed.

When enough healthy tissues were formed during the 'wait and watch' period of over two months, I was operated on again to graft skin over the exposed wound. Skin from both of my thighs were taken in slices and surgically placed over the newly formed tissues after debridement.

With the operation over, it was another 11 days waiting before finding out if the graft had taken. My movement was totally restricted and I was confined to my bed during that period of excruciating pain and anxiety. If the graft failed, then I had very little chance for another operation since my fragile body no longer had enough skin to cover up the wound.

After 11 days of praying and hoping, the chief surgeon and other doctors came and removed the bandages. I saw signs of satisfaction on their faces as they inspected my leg, and I was very happy when they said that the graft had set in, much beyond their expectation. The operation had been successful and I was relieved from the thought of being attached with a prosthetic limb (artificial leg) - a sad, undisclosed thought that had been the cause of much anxiety and fear, from the day of admission.

I remained in the hospital for another two months and got discharged finally, after nearly six months.

## *When normal is abnormal...*

I had been discharged with advice to undergo physiotherapy and daily dressing. With not being able to extend my leg straight, I could not walk normally.  Part of the wound was taking time to heal, therefore, I had to dress the wound daily.  I decided it was better not to go home where I had no access to proper medical care.  I went and stayed at my sister's place in a bigger town where I thought I had a better chance of a fast recovery but, unfortunately that was not to be. Having access to a better health care system in the urban town also meant easy access to drugs, and particularly alcohol which is sold unchecked in many outlets, pubs, night clubs, hotels and restaurants.

After five to six months of my stay, I started taking alcohol with an excuse of easing the pain in my leg and for sleeplessness.  I never realised that it was yet another plan of the devil to take away my life that had somehow survived. I had stopped taking drugs altogether for over one and half years and so far, alcohol had never been a big issue in my life. Just like with drugs, the unseen forces of adversary encouraged me by instilling in my mind that I could consume alcohol in limit, being beset with pain and that I could easily give up as soon as my problem was over. So, just like the fool I had been with drugs, I started consuming liquor.

Looking back, I realised I needed a prop in life. Like someone who has a weak leg and needing a crutch to help walk day by day, I was needing drugs or alcohol as my daily prop.

What was deemed as having a normal drink, became abnormal. Going from casual drinking to absorbing myself in it. Days of drinking would turn into a month at a time, then I was needing to take a 'drink' to keep me sober. Until, I would drink again too much and then be found lying outside a drinking den, on a roadside, blacked out.

Somehow, I sensed that in blacking out that someday I would waken up and, in that moment, realise, my life was over. I would awaken more than likely in hell, never to have another chance to change my direction in life. This habit didn't augur well with my health and with those people who finally discovered my new habit.

Soon, all our family members and relatives came to know about it. They chastised and advised me in many different ways about why I should not take alcohol, but all their kind advice and admonishes fell onto deaf ears. Instead of taking heed, I continued drinking, and when I desired euphoria lacking only with alcohol, I upped the 'ante' by taking drugs on occasion.

Gradually, I began to tread along the same old, 'god-forsaken' path which I thought, I had forsaken for all good times.

I procured drugs once in four to five months and abused it for two to three days. This intermittent usage of drugs with alcohol and all other vices that come along with them brought great discord and disharmony in our family. My presence, with my evil habits, was unacceptable to all the people I was associated with, except the devil himself.

As I continued with my habits, our family members, having tried and lost all ways and means to put an end to my vices, urged me to go to a prayer centre. I was reluctant to go so I kept procrastinating. Then one day, after an argument with family members, under the influence of alcohol, I was compelled to leave for the centre.

## *Who said the fight is easy?...*

Dad and Mum accompanied me on my first trip to the prayer centre. Dad left the same day while Mum stayed for a night and went back. Before she left, Mum and I met Pastor Luvukhu, the God-anointed caretaker of the centre who gave me seven days to fast and pray (36 hours dry fast, six hours break cycle). I wondered how I was going to spend those days. I was in poor health and my leg problem still persisted. As such, during services I'd sit at the back far behind all other people.

During those seven days I was more conscious of other people around me and could not do much soul-searching. On the last day, after having packed my meagre belongings, I went to meet a counsellor, a woman endowed with spiritual gifts, to seek her blessings.

Towards the end of her prayer she changed her tone and in plain, clear utterances said that God wanted me to stay for another two weeks! Then, she ended her prayer and asked if I was willing to continue my fast as instructed by God through the Holy Spirit. I was hesitant, but to my own surprise I said that I would give it a try.

I let my family members know of the development and unrolled my bedding. The 14 day extension I got turned out to be of great blessing because I could pray better and also learn many new things.

Towards the end, my health improved and I gained more confidence. I could also promise myself that, I would try my best to give up my bad habits before I finally left.

However, it wasn't a strong commitment which I could abide by.

I slowly started to drift away to my old despicable ways. I stealthily started to take alcohol and the habit stuck. I would be sober for days and weeks together but would fail to resist the temptation sometimes. This self-betrayal continued and I was almost back to where I was before going to the centre.

After several months, my sister suggested that I go back to centre. I agreed but went alone this time. I was given five days by the same pastor, during which time I fasted, prayed for God's forgiveness and made new promises.

On the last day of the fast, the pastor prayed and reminded me saying, "If I say I won't do it - then I shouldn't do it." Why should I keep on fooling myself and my parents? He then told me to remain blessed and under God's grace.

I returned from the centre and remained as good and 'clean' as I could be. After a few weeks the urge to take alcohol kicked in, and I succumbed to the temptation saying that it would be for the last time. Having drunk, I knew I had broken my promises and had become a backslider - ever sliding deeper into the dark corners of my own grave.

This cycle of making and breaking promises continued and soon I found myself in a much worse condition than I'd ever been. Discouragement, frustration, self-pity and disillusionment became my constant companion. I would often lay awake past midnight, engulfed with anxiety and insecurity. Peace, I had none, and love I could give to none, as I hardly had any love for myself.

## Shattered dreams...

Almost everyone had lost hope in me. Sending me to the prayer centre had backfired. Family members stopped talking about fasting and prayers, and they all had a valid reason, for how long would I fool myself, my family and God.

On my part, I felt it too shameful to mention God. I recoiled into my own shell of greater disillusionment and utter helplessness, all the time thinking how I could go so wrong in my life. Deep in my heart, I knew that God never intended me to be what I had become; rather He had created me for a definite purpose.

Year after year of drug abuse and alcoholism had almost taken away my sanity, and my wisdom was flickering out. I did desire to be some value to others, for I knew my values and my worth, but having not used God-gifted talents, I had not only betrayed the reason behind my creation and my own understanding, but also shattered my life and crushed all hopes and dreams of loved ones, thus all the values and knowledge I had gathered along my life's journey remained like the proverbial lit lamp under a basket.

Around this time, my sister got in contact with a pastor of a local fellowship, a God-inspired acquaintance filled with the Holy Spirit and took me to meet him. After a casual introduction, he asked me what I wished to become, and even before I could answer completely, he told me to go to a prayer centre for a seven day fast.

I had, by then, given up on the thought of going even to a prayer centre, and instead was planning to go back home in a few days, but when I was asked if I was willing, I slowly nodded in agreement. He said a prayer for me and my sister and asked us to make haste to go.

A day later, I went to the centre with a heavy heart and a guilty conscience, while realising in some corner of my depraved mind that, it could be my last chance. I met the pastor, helplessly filled with shame. He was not pleased to see me back in that doomed state. He pitied my condition, and after praying told me to fast for seven days adding he would see me after that!

I knew that I was laden with an even heavier physical, mental and spiritual burden. God-given understanding had almost abandoned me and I found it difficult to gather my thoughts whenever I spoke. I realised that the wisdom and knowledge I once possessed were being taken away from me, and I became fearful of becoming insane.

It was no coincidence when, on the first day of my fast, I received a message from my sister saying it had been prophesied that a male youth from our colony was going to become mad. It was also no coincidence when on my first night I so vividly dreamt of two black birds trying to claw and peck away on my head. I believed from the core of my heart that the prophecy had been told about me.

Even before coming to the centre, I had been beset with sleepless nights for many days. My body would be so tired and my eyes would become heavy, yet, I would awaken suddenly with unexplained fear suddenly as I was dozing off.

The same episode continued even at the centre and I found myself awake while others slept in peace. I began to feel scared to close my eyes even during daytime because I would see or dream horrendous things. I prayed to God to help me sleep in peace but I would awaken with the same feeling of fear. So, in the silence of the darkness, hours after midnight I crept into the prayer hall and sought the Lord's mercy and grace. Still, normal sleep eluded me for the next few days and nights.

However, in that sleepless and restless period, I got the opportunity in solitude to pray and cry out to Jesus with deep introspection. I asked Him to teach me how to approach Him and what I should say in front of Him. He let me remember my sins and other long-forgotten wrongs done unto others, for which I had to repent.

Soon, I got into the habit of repenting and making confessions, and as much as I confessed with contrite spirit, I found peace and could gradually sleep normally by the fourth night of my fast.

Towards the end of my fast, it dawned on me that I was the greatest fool among all other fools in this whole world. How truly reckless and irresponsible I'd been so far in my life and that, if Judas Iscariot had betrayed Jesus Christ once, (Luke 22:4-6, 48, Matthew 26: 14-16) then I have betrayed my own Saviour a thousand times.

On my last day, I met the pastor who prayed for me and warned me about the temptations that would come along my way within no time. He told me to return to the centre when the going got tough. I left with a light heart, knowing that the spirit of insanity and death had left me, at least for a while.

# CHAPTER 7

# *The battle starts...*

Not long after, I returned to the prayer centre because I knew I was still like a small child needing constant care and feeding in spiritual life. The outside world was still raw for my small, budding faith.

I was prescribed five days, the first three days of which were spent without much progress. I was simply following the normal ritual and practices of the centre without any spiritual insight.

On the fourth day when I realised that I was going to return home empty-handed, my pride and self-righteousness at the thought of having overcome some of my vices had put a stumbling block in my spiritual progress. I needed to cast off this thought completely from my mind and go to the Lord in all humility and with all my mind, body and soul. That night, I went to the prayer hall after watching everyone sleep. It was empty and quiet, and I found it better since I could talk to God freely, in isolation.

I entered the hall and knelt down in humble supplication. As I started to pray, I experienced such a strange feeling that I had never felt before. I began to feel scared, for no apparent reason, and felt as if darkness had engulfed me from behind. Suddenly, I heard noises, like someone entering the hall and imagined him standing near me, just watching and saying nothing. My strength weakened and I could only mumble away my prayer incoherently, in fear and confusion. I realised that neither one was from God.

Our God is not an author of confusion, (1 Corinthians 14:33); and fear is one of the most powerful weapons used by the devil against God's people in strategic spiritual warfare.

Under normal circumstances, I might have mumbled 'Amen' and hurried away to the room filled with other people, but that was exactly what my enemy wanted me to do. I knew that it was a spiritual battle, and since my enemy was not of flesh and blood, I should fight him in the Spirit, but with what weapons could I overcome my unseen enemy? In my arsenal, laying seldom used and rusting away with time, were the weapons I could still use: The Bible (God's Word), the Blood of Christ, the Name of Jesus, Worship, Prayer, Spiritual gifts, humility, obedience, fasting, music, etc.

Considering my situation, I chose God's Word and the Name of Jesus to be a better choice as my weapons. For the first time in my life, I exercised the power vested upon me by God, through the Holy Spirit, and started waging a lone spiritual battle with the invisible enemy by taking the Name of Jesus Christ and claiming aloud the following Scriptures:

*'He who believes and is baptized will be saved; but he who does not believe will be condemned. And these signs will follow those who believe: In My name they will cast out demons; they will speak with new tongues; they will take up serpents; and if they drink anything deadly, it will by no means hurt them; they will lay hands on the sick, and they will recover.'* Mark 16:17-18

*'Therefore submit to God. Resist the devil and he will flee from you.'* James 4:7

*'Behold, I give you the authority to trample on serpents and scorpions, and over all the power of the enemy, and nothing shall by any means hurt you.'* Luke 10:19

As I would read those verses again and again. I would begin to rebuke in louder and stronger terms, the spirit of fear and all other evil spirits. Proclaiming the Name of Jesus Christ and His precious blood over me.

Slowly, but assuredly, I began to feel a gentle calm descend over me, replacing the darkness that had enveloped me. As I continued to rebuke and cast off the devil, my heartbeat returned to normal and finally, after invoking God's grace and the power of the Holy Spirit, I felt all feelings of fear dissipate and I felt at peace.

I imagined that the Lord Jesus was standing before me, keeping watch over me and I knew that I could now tell Him everything I wanted freely and with my entire being. I began by repenting and confessing for all the intentional and unintentional wrongs I'd so far committed. Then, I made a plea to the Lord to never let me leave the centre without having received His blessing.

I lay prostrate, stretched out with face to the ground, in submission to the Lord and continued with my plea, telling God of my weaknesses and backsliding and prayed for the armour of God, to be put on me as soon as I left the centre, that I may stand strong wherever I be.

While praying, it suddenly dawned on me that I, in all of my previous visits to the centre had never made a firm, binding covenant with the Lord. I went into deep self-introspection and realised that I was, 'a branch that bears not fruit.' (John 15:2) I should have seen death long ago, but simply because of His immense love I have been kept alive.

My life's validity had already expired due to drugs and alcohol addiction. However, without my knowledge, it had been recharged with new breath of life, in the mercy and grace of the Almighty God.

Realising this, I thanked the Lord with all my heart and made a commitment that, I wouldn't abuse drugs or take alcohol ever again, and whatever little good knowledge and wisdom remained in my life,

I'd use it for the purpose of good only, and that, since it's His gifted life to me, I would allow Him to nurture, support and guide me all through life's ups and downs. After making this covenant, for the first time in my life, I silently left the prayer hall and went to sleep in peaceful resolve.

On the last day of my fast, I was privileged to meet Rev. Dr. Vikheshe Chishi, Chairman of the Withee Bible College. He is a distant relative who happened to be there at the centre during my allotted time. He gave me the much-needed encouragement and warned me in no simple terms, saying if I went against my commitment then it would mean hell for me. His presence and messages delivered on two occasions during his stay at the centre gave new impetus to my commitment to stop abusing drugs particularly. Later, after having received his inspiration, Godly advices and blessings in prayer, I took his leave.

I left the centre that same afternoon and returned to my sister's place and tried to focus my mind on writing my testimonial, instead of spending my time and resources on my vices. Within days, I went home, bought a book and a pen and placed them in the hands of my Mum. After telling her of my intention, I asked her to pray about it. Soon, I was scribbling away... within eight days I completed the first draft.

## Staying steadfast...

Life was not rosy or easy even after making and abiding by the covenant. In fact, life was much more difficult to carry on since I found myself living in an entirely different world, with different people who knew me only as a drug addict without hope of any change.

It was only God, my family, and a few close friends who knew about my decision. I still had to prove myself and bend the pointing fingers of those people who jeered at me and tagged me as a social outcast.

I knew I should do something meaningful in order to be counted and accepted by our society. Then it dawned on me: I need not be bothered about other people's opinion of me; if I honour the covenant and live by its principles then ultimately things will change for the better. People's perception will alter, and my humble self won't have the need to prove anything to anybody. With this understanding, I left my critics in the hands of God and moved on to play my committed role on the stage of sobriety, in all honesty.

The need and the wish to complete my medical degree formed as the foremost priority in my mind, therefore I explained my desire to my parents in detail who gave me their consent. With their blessing, I left home and travelled down south to my college in Visakhapatnam, hoping and praying that I would be given a chance to continue and complete my degree.

I met our Principal and the staff and made a self-representation, requesting permission for continuation and completion of my M.B;B.S degree. The Principal told me that I was not eligible to continue my studies in the college unless the university permitted; for which I was to make my representation in writing to the Vice-Chancellor, NTR University of Health Sciences, situated in another city, Vijayawada.

I was utterly disappointed. I never thought that I was no longer a student of Andhra Medical College, the premier institute I considered as my college! Moreover, I had not brought enough money to travel to another city.

In a tearful plea, I shared my thoughts and predicament with the Principal. Feeling concerned he told me that he would get my application and other required documents attested and put into words for me and also that, I could send my letter of representation to the university from the post office.

I felt some weight of disappointment lift from my shoulders, and made haste to write the application, arrange all the required documents and got them attested from the Principal. When it was done I had my letter sent from the post office.

The next day, I headed back for home disheartened, but with a flicker of hope lighting the path of my medical career.

Back at home, while I awaited a letter of intimation from the university, I began to revise and edit the first book draft again which I wished to get printed and released soon.

I also started to write articles on drugs and alcohol, socioeconomic, religious and political affairs of our state. Soon, I was contributing to the dailies on a regular basis, but my priority at that point of time was to complete the editing work and have my book printed and released.

I finished my task of revision and editing, however due to financial constraints I could not get it printed on time. I had no source of income, nor was my family in a position to help me financially. So, I started searching for the means to have my book printed, but hardly found any support.

The people who could have helped me looked at me through the lens of self-righteousness and judged me based on my past and shied away from helping me.

As days passed by, I began to feel discouraged. Here I was, trying my best to reap the benefits of the covenant by going to the church regularly, accepting invitations and sharing my testimony in various churches, conferences, youth and students' seminars, then contributing to the newspapers to create awareness on drug abuse and alcoholism in our society, but I found no avenues opening for me. Moreover, the flicker of hope lighting the path of my medical career seemed to be fading out. It was already six months since I returned home after posting my application to the university from the post office, but I was yet to receive their feedback.

CHAPTER 8

# *When it's time to say goodbye...*

In the midst of all the discouragements, doubts, anxiety and confusion, my beloved Dad fell ill, beset with multi-organ disease, from which he couldn't recover.

The night before his death, I went to meet him during visiting hours in the Intensive Care Unit (ICU). He was no longer able to speak. I knew he was dying - when that moment was, only God knew. I held his hand and told him that he could leave and the place where he was going to was far better than our world; that even though he was far away from Mum, he need not worry because she would understand. I promised I would try my best to keep his name and honour alive.

I then bowed my head and trying to hold back the pain in my heart of my Dad about to pass away I asked, "Would you please forgive me for all my wrongs and bad habits?"

Remaining unresponsive, I pleaded for his forgiveness for having gone astray and causing him grief by not allowing him to eat/savour the fruit of the tree in me he so lovingly planted, nurtured, and looked upon to bear many fruits.

He clasped his fingers around my hand and gave me a firm grip. My eyes welled up and I lost utterance.

Two nurses came in, visiting time was over, as I silently wept. Politely they told me to leave, but instead of leaving, I still held on to my Dad's hand and started to pray. After I had said; 'Amen,' I tenderly released Dad's hand and turned around to leave. Much to my surprise, I saw the two nurses still standing behind me with their heads bowed. I knew I had broken the protocol of the ICU and they had every right to scold and send me out, but instead they chose to support me in prayer.

I left the ICU and kept watch over him in spirit and silent prayers as I rested my anxiety-ridden mind and stressed-out body in the waiting lounge that was filled with sombre-cast attendants of other critical patients. By the dawn of a new day, my sister reached the ICU to work her shift of watching Dad and I headed for the guesthouse where we were residing temporarily. I collapsed on the bed exhausted and was soon fast asleep.

An hour later I received a call from ICU, asking me to be present immediately. On arrival, I saw my sister facing the wall, standing and weeping silently near the ICU doorway. I rushed past her and the sight that greeted me was like living out a nightmare.

A doctor and two male nurses were trying to revive my Dad through CPR (Cardio-Pulmonary Resuscitation). I told them to stop and keep away. They obliged and got off from the bed; I stepped in and checked Dad's pulse and other vital signs. My beloved Dad was no more.

I consulted with the ICU Chief for making necessary arrangements and left to meet my sister. She was weeping audibly in between making calls. I rubbed her shoulder and told her that we could cry our hearts out for days, even weeks, but only after reaching home that was a day's journey away from where we were. She soaked up my words and sniffed up her emotions, then started calling up contacts while I took care of paperwork and other formalities. When it was all done, we left the hospital where Dad had been an in-patient for 28 days and headed for our home town.

Dad's sojourn on earth had ended and his mortal remains reached home the next morning and was buried the same day as per our custom.

# *Career change…*

Six months after my Dad's demise, the printed edition of my debut book was released locally. Not long after, I found myself busy sharing my testimony and exhorting the youths, in particular, on alcohol and drug addiction by invitation, from various institutes, organisations and churches.

I realise today, that it was one of the most blessed periods of my life and I should have remained happy without feeling worried or anxious, but at that time, I was more worried than being happy. I would feel happy and grateful to God for the opportunity to stand in front of other people and share my story, but after every programme I would go back home and ponder away in the solitude of my room; anxiety and insecurities would crowd my mind and the little happiness I gained in my day time would be lost by the time I slept late at night. Also, age was catching up faster on me than I thought, and I was still jobless.

The university seemed to have died out on me, and yet I had to keep my commitment I made with my Dad. A week before he died, Dad told me, in no uncertain terms, that his utmost desire and wish was for me to complete my medical degree. I had replied that I would try my best to fulfil his wish.

However, as ignorant and selfish as this might sound, here I was, keeping myself busy for others and fulfilling their wishes while doing nothing to fulfil Dad's utmost desire, or for my dream of becoming a doctor, albeit belatedly. Dad's death was still fresh in my mind and the grief behind his loss was eating away into my peace and happiness. Therefore, I finally made up my mind to meet the Vice-Chancellor in person, and left for Vijayawada, where my university was located, after informing Mum and my siblings.

Three days after reaching the city I got an appointment to meet the Vice-Chancellor and I gathered all the necessary documents before meeting him in his chamber. He read my representation and attached documents and told me to wait in the visitor's lounge while he discussed my matter with his Secretary and the Registrar of the university.

After a few minutes I was ushered into his office again. I was told that I had overstayed my vacation and according to the rules of the university, I was no longer eligible to pursue my medical degree; and that he couldn't do anything to help me.

My heart sank and I almost cried, but I composed myself and in all humility with folded hands, I requested him to kindly consider my application, at least on humanitarian grounds, also adding that it was my late father's last and ultimate wish which I sincerely desired to carry out. He looked into my tear-filled eyes and told me that he'd see if he could do anything, then suggested that I go back home and wait for his letter.

I thanked the Vice-Chancellor and the Registrar and left the university compound. That same night I bid 'adieu' to the city and travelled back home, not realising that it would be the last time I'd be visiting them... for my medical career.

## *Medico turned writer and poet...*

I returned home safe and sound and gave my report to my Mum and siblings. A few weeks after settling down, I found myself following the same routine. I'd accept the invitation from the churches, colleges and other organisations and share my testimony; exhort the youths and the young students, then in my leisure I'd write articles and send them to the editors for publication in their newspapers. Days passed into months but nothing was forthcoming from the university office. They seemed to have forgotten his given word to me.

I was becoming frustrated and feeling utterly low; my life continued, but the hope I carried in my spirit was diminishing with each passing day. God seemed to have gone silent and remained Himself aloof to my problems and heartaches. I was hurting... feeling lonely and depressed.

One winter night, I wondered and pondered deep into how and where I might have possibly gone wrong; and if it was worth the wait.

I realised that I was yet to fully overcome; that I had been holding onto my past regrets and would ofttimes go into hiding inside the safety of my own cell... building layers upon layers of walls for frustrations, discouragement and with every setback or failure in my life.

I realised that I needed to come out from my shell and open up to the world in order to get rid of the past regrettable vestiges from my life and be accepted by society, for the sake of my future and my family.

That cold winter night of Christmas season, while my family slept in our humble home, I walked out from my warm cosy bed, wrapped my already shivering body in a woollen traditional shawl and took a short walk across the street from our house. The streets of our town were lit up and sparkling with Christmas lights. They looked like diamonds scintillating and sparkling in the light.

As I watched the spectacular display of lights, a soft and tender voice clearly rang out saying, "You are a Diamond of Dust."

I looked around but didn't see anyone. A voice rang out again, "You are a Diamond of Dust!"

With the voice still ringing in my ears I headed back to the cosy comfort of my bed, and pondered on what this voice meant, and finally it dawned on me, that I was indeed so much like useless dust, but the voice was telling me that I could sparkle like a diamond, provided I allow the Light to work its wonder on me.

I realised then, like the people in the Bible, a voice none other than the Spirit of God had spoken and I was to obey. I needed to come out from my dark confines and let the rays of the Light do its work. The dust that I was, needed to present myself to Jesus, the Light, and scintillate with its rays in order to sparkle like a diamond.

I desired much to sparkle like a diamond, and therefore in the middle of the night of that cold wintry Christmas, I resolved to break down the walls and come out from my self-built cell. Saying my humble prayer and thanking our Saviour for coming into the world for someone like me, I slept in a peaceful resolve.

The following morning, I felt as if there were a river of words flowing from my inner being and with that, I started composing poems. After such a gap of nothing happening, it would seem now when I look back, the river within me had hit a wall but in my brokenness and with God speaking, that wall broke and the power of His Spirit was bursting through me. I was writing my own quotes, short articles, poetries, acronym-based one-liners etc. and sharing them with others through social media, particularly on Facebook.

Through time, I had made friends with scores of good people who supported and encouraged me to keep writing. Some of them suggested that I should create my own page since plagiarism was not unknown, and my intellectual property could be stolen by others, but I didn't even know how to use Facebook properly. So, I left it at that, and kept on with my writing.

Previously, I would spend most of my time scripting articles on drugs and alcohol related issues, socioeconomic, religious and political affairs of the state, and fictions. My interest gradually shifted to composing poems, penning my own quotes and that was because I could release my feelings and emotions through my lines and rhymes, finding relief to some extent.

Time passed by, and I made even more friends through social media. Others also conveyed to me the same idea of having my own page created. I finally decided to put their suggestions into effect and created 'Reflections - A. Anato Swu.'

I tried my best to keep it alive and vibrant. Today, if my page serves any purpose, then the credit should go to all my friends who have been there to inspire, encourage and support me.

I had, by then, made many good virtual friends, but in real life I hardly had anyone whom I could call a good friend for all seasons. Therefore, even though my life was active and vibrant in the virtual world, I had to battle it out with my loneliness and insecurities once I went offline. This pathetic condition was aggravated by doubts and anxiety over my medical career. Each new day was spent in eager expectation of a feedback from the university, but when, even after six months of a 'wait and watch' period, I did not receive any letter, my doubts turned into a confirmation, that the door to my medical ambition was closed.

This confirmation brought depression and sadness into my life. As much as I desired and tried to overcome any negative thoughts and feelings, I seemed to be fighting a battle that was already lost. I couldn't share, nor did I wish to disclose, my pathetic condition to others - friends or family members. Thus, I became a victim of negative attitudes and unhealthy emotions.

Outwardly, I presented myself as a person keeping well in all aspects of life, but inwardly, only God and I knew how much I suffered and wept.

There were times when I would script poems with tears streaming down my cheeks and times when my anger compelled me to write articles or anything that served as an outlet to my ire and frustrations. Mostly, it was in the silence of the night, that I gave words to my thoughts and feelings, while others slept happily, or without care.

My days turned shorter, my nights longer and in betwixt, my life and my world became dark, full of confusion. The little joy I could garner in the day time would be snatched away by depression and a hoard of negative feelings in the night time. I would sometimes think of giving up, but there would be this soft, still Voice calling out my name, and telling me to express my feelings instead.

The Voice would tell me what and how to write, and I would just follow the lead. So even though, I knew not where my life was headed for, I kept on writing.

At times I would ponder did David know he was called to be a king before he was anointed? There was young David the shepherd, in the fields caring and protecting the sheep to the point where he killed a lion and a bear. (1 Samuel 17).

Then a day came while he was still in the field just being faithful to his Dad's orders when the prophet Samuel calls to see him and David's life was changed forever. Or did Moses know the path God had for him while being raised under Pharaoh's house, until the tree burnt and a Voice spoke from it. (Exodus 3).

When I read Scripture, I have concluded when God seeks to bring one into a new place in Him, He gives that person an encounter of Himself, whether through the reality of God or one of His servants who knows His reality. I was about to find that out and this poem is dedicated to that person who was about to change my life.

## *My Beautiful Red Rose*

Blooming rich and rare in God's own garden,
Like t'e first rose by the cool waters of Eden;
Behold her, dancing happy in t'e gentle wind,
My beautiful red rose of t'e most pretty kind.

Her fragrance angels love to wear,
Her bloom to sight so lovely dear,
Her stalk ever strong and unbending,
Her leaves evergreen, unwithering.

Care and tended by the sole Gardener;
Watered by Heaven's blessed shower;
Ever watched aft'r by love so personal,
My lovely Rose blooms for one and all.

Layers after layers of scarlet virgin petals,
She opens up for the pleasure of mortals.
Yet lesser does she desire of her bloom,
That greater be His glory over e'ery gloom.

Pollen from her age-graced ripen'd body,
Spread forth as essence for ill's remedy;
Scatter'd by her butterfly to world distant,
Her memory we'll carry in mind constant.

Pluck her not but let her bloom undefiled.
Bloom of grace and charity quite unrivalled;
She lives in simulation of the greatest love,
That we all be blest as desired from above.

# CHAPTER 9

## *Just Mama...*

Maureen Wylie (addressed as Mama from here on) came into my life out of the blue from Facebook... Just when my life was at its lowest ebb, and hope of a happy life and future seemed to be fading, God chose someone from half a world away to calm the waters that was rocking my boat so hard and rough. Had God not sent Mama, then my rocking boat would have thrown me far out into the seas and I would have drowned in the waters of despair and sorrow. I would have been gone without leaving even a trace of a good memory to be cherished by those I'd have left behind.

When the world had rejected me, and couldn't even give me a second chance to continue my studies despite my humble pleas, Mama brought a beautiful message about 'The God of the Second Chance,' and this second chance concerned 'life' itself - my life which should have been snubbed out decades ago but had been extended through His grace, and it came unasked for. I was made to understand the importance and the ocean-vast difference between 'my ambition' and 'my life.'

# The God of 'The Second Chance'

*There are times when the sinners silently weep,*
*Finding themselves drowning, sinking deep,*
*In the murky waters of worldly pleasure,*
*They once loved to swim in at leisure,*
*To exercise their God-given freewill,*
*With a choice that would only kill-*
*Both the mortal body and soul,*
*And parcel them to Sheol.*

*It's their heart that weeps,*
*Whilst the world gently sleeps.*
*Sin-stained dream awakens them;*
*Past memory only spells ugly shame;*
*The soul's gut-wrenching cries of protest,*
*O'er the envisioned place for its eternal rest,*
*Keep them awake-wishing and longing for rescue.*
*But finding none they weep and weep as their due.*

*Sometimes their weepin' heart is seen by the Lord,*
*Whose love, and grace, and mercy cannot afford,*
*To be overshadowed by the sins of the world.*
*Thus He chooses instead to love and scold,*
*And gives strength and comfort to them.*
*That they mayn't drown in their shame,*
*But for death, a new life exchange,*
*From God of the second chance.*

Soon, a marathon exchange of letters ensued. For the first time in my life I willed myself for God, to love and be loved, taught, chastised, and also learn the lessons through His handmaiden I had not even met. Every conversation between Mama and I, ended with a gem of a lesson which I collected and treasured in the atrium of my heart.

Through Mama I was honoured to befriend her esteemed husband Maurice Wylie - a revelatory speaker, a gifted writer, and a man of God endowed with spiritual gifts of knowledge, wisdom, discernment, understanding and vision - to name a few.

A few days after our paths crossed, I trusted him enough to disclose my past life, sharing in brief how I had wasted the better part of my youth and my medical career on drugs and alcohol addiction. He read into my life under God and told me to never consider having wasted anything; and that even if I had failed to become a medical doctor, I could become a *Doctor of life.*

After our conversation, I pondered hard on what he had said, and I realised how ignorantly wrong and silly I had been to have carried such thoughts with me all those years. I was immensely encouraged, particularly when it dawned on me that I could use my past experiences to help and encourage those lost souls treading the darkened path of drug abuse and alcoholism.

A few days later, I was blessed to be introduced to 'THE GOD OF NEW BEGINNINGS' by Mama, who made me understand that I could leave my past behind - all regrets, heartaches, pains, remorse... and start a new beginning in His Name.

# *The God of New Beginnings*

*Walking along the lonely, dreary road;*
*Alien from the path you once trod;*
*Leaving behind the good guide;*
*Lured away to the dark side.*

*Knowing not where the road leads;*
*Ignorant of the sign that reads-*
*"Destination Hell" for souls,*
*For whom the bell tolls.*

*All the while the adversary smiles,*
*As you cover the cursed miles.*
*Till you discover it's too late,*
*To escape your ugly fate.*

*But God does keep watch and cry,*
*Over your soul that's gone dry.*
*For His mercy angels plead-*
*Seeking for grace to lead.*

*Saints too, make their plea and pray,*
*For you to find back your way,*
*Into the path of Truth and Light-*
*To dying soul's delight!*

*Tear-filled prayers move the Lord,*
*And in His grace and His Word,*
*He stretches forth His Hand,*
*Ere you turn the final bend.*

*Halted from your Journey to Hell,*
*You'd return with a Story to tell,*
*If only you'd give your hand,*
*To God of the beginning and the end.*

*His love ends and vexes evil plans,*
*Puts to nought dark designs,*
*He is, for spirit grooming,*
*God of new beginnings!*

I knew I had begun my new journey, and if I wouldn't stray off course or become distracted then this journey was going to take me to wonderful destinations. I was excited and immensely grateful to the Lord and to the blessed God-chosen couple. Regularly Mama would enlighten me to the ways of God, opening my spiritual eyes to new lessons of healthy, spiritual living which I never had heard before.

Day after day, passed by; lesson after lesson I learned by heart. Then one day, a thought struck me: I had a natural mother, one who gave birth to me; was it possible for me to have a spiritual mother? My heart said 'why not?' And from that day, after informing Mama Maureen and my Mum, and with their consent, I accepted and started honouring Mama as my spiritual mother.

Soon after, Mama introduced and got me enrolled in 'THE MAGNIFICENT SCHOOL.' I wondered what kind of school that might possibly be, and she explained that it was a school where we would learn and digest the Word and apply it in our lives. Where we would spend time in prayers and meditation on the Scriptures; where the fruits of the Spirit could be harvested in the presence of the Lord. Where we could exercise our faith in 'the gym' equipped with all the necessary 'work-out machines, materials and equipment.' It was a school where Our Lord Jesus Christ was the Headmaster and Chief Mentor.

As she elaborated on the facilities available in the school, I felt the express need to start attending the classes in my heart. I promised myself to be a regular student, but due to my own shortcomings and circumstances, I couldn't hold on to my promise and absented myself for days or weeks together.

Tied to the tough situations, my heart would ache and feel ashamed too, but I couldn't command enough courage to return. Mama would always find out and call me up or send messages of concern laced in love and grace; and I would follow her back to the 'School.'

One early summer morning, as we were chatting, Mama asked if I would allow her to help support me. I was pleasantly baffled, and couldn't reply immediately. I turned emotional, and took some silent moments to think and understand, composed myself, and asked her why she would ever want to support someone like me who she had not even met? She said it was a matter that God placed on her heart, and that she wanted to support my writing. With tears of gratitude and joy, I gave her my consent. Since then, Mama has been supporting me with what she calls as her 'Love Gift'. I could never believe that such a beautiful thing would ever happen in my life, and in all humility and much gratefulness, I thank the Good Lord for Mama and her soul-partner every day.

As our journey continued I began to understand the power of Love through what Mama taught me and practised herself. She truly loves our Lord with all her heart, mind and soul; and her life and deeds only reflect the 'Love of God'. Her financial support doesn't have any strings attached. I came to realise early that I was not under any obligation for being a recipient of her help. She explained that I was never to look upon her gift as anything other than her sowing into God's Kingdom.

Our journey together in God, was possible because of her love and tears for humanity. Clothed in humility, she would always try to inspire, encourage and edify my spirit.

Unknown to Mama, she became my inspiration, and almost all of my poetries, quotes, and articles that had been written after we started our journey bears the trademark of her life and love. The magnanimity of her love and concern for others could be gauged to some extent by a small but significant incident that follows.

Over half a year into our journey together in spirit and in His love, one sunny day, Mama asked if I could do her a favour. When I promptly replied in affirmative, she thanked me and told me to go to a florist, buy ten stalks of red roses, and give it to my dear Mum. I was pleasantly surprised, but at the same time, I found myself in a fixed state since our small town had no florist, and also my Mum was away from home.

Still, I assured her that it would be done as per her wish, whilst planning to get the flowers from a bigger town.

A couple of days later Mama wanted to know if her roses had been delivered, because she felt that my Mum needed love, support, encouragement and prayers in generous measure. I replied in negative saying that my Mum was still away.

A week passed and Mum returned from her journey. That same evening, I remembered that I had noticed some weeks earlier while going to the church, lovely roses blooming where the local army battalion headquarters was located.

Not wanting to be noticed, my nephew and I approached the headquarters and pulling out a pair of scissors, I carefully clipped the rose stalks of the lovely blooms.

After our job was done we were on our way home, when the checkpoint guard stopped us and inquired about the flowers and started scolding us.

I told my nephew to proceed homeward and after seeing him at a safe distance, I turned to the guard and apologised, adding that it would never happen again. I also introduced my Dad who was an officer in the same battalion where he was serving currently. On learning who my Dad was, his manner changed noticeably. He asked why I had plucked the flowers without permission. I simply told him that it was meant for my Mum.

He let me go without saying any more. On reaching home I arranged the flowers in an old, but still usable, transparent gift wrapper in the best way I could and presented it to my Mum telling her from whom and for what reasons the lovely red blooms have been gifted for. She was pleasantly shocked when I told her what the red roses conveyed, because that was exactly what she needed at that time.

Mum was away for her health problem and the treatment regimen had been hard on her aged health, then also unhealthy circumstances prevailing in our family, was robbing her off the little joy she had. Love, encouragement and prayerful support were the unseen, but invaluable things she had needed most above all other things at that time. I left her with the roses in her room after taking few pics.

A few minutes later she started praying, taking the name of Mama to the Lord in humble acknowledgement of her love. She pronounced Mama's name (Maureen) as "Maulyn" and Ireland as 'eyeland.' It reminded me of that day in school when my Dad corrected me for my pronunciation, but I knew God would understand, He reads our hearts more than our words.

I sent some of the pictures I'd taken to Mama, explaining my shortcomings, said my prayer of gratitude, closed the chapter of my day and went to sleep.

Early next morning I woke up to be greeted with a beautiful message from Mama saying that she was overwhelmed by my act of love, and that she could never nor would she attempt to try and improve on it, because she couldn't.

Her message humbled me and left me speechless. I could only say, "Thank you Lord, thank you Mama."

To Mama and her 'bestie' as she calls Maurice, her husband, love was all about sharing and giving which they practised in their daily lives. One afternoon in hot summer, I received a bulky parcel sent by Mama through courier service. I opened it and saw that it was a Bible - Mama's personal study Bible! Thick and heavy.

I tried to reason out the purpose behind the parcel that also contained a beautiful wooden photo frame. Then it suddenly dawned on me, in my past, I had never etched the Word of God in the tablet of my heart, nor did I have any interest to read the Bible, and therefore I was prone to backslide. Had I carried the Bible along my life's journey, I wouldn't have caused such pain and sadness to my family and myself.

Mama discovered the reason behind my failures, and she desired that I should not only read but also study and digest the Word and apply it in my day-to-day life. Today, Mama's Bible is treasured as one of the most priceless gifts that I've ever received in my life.

Not long after, another parcel arrived, this time from her bestie, Maurice Wylie. It contained two books: 'A Bride Prepared' written by himself. The book serves as an eye-opener to readers to new insights and revelations. It exposes the hidden truths and lies which would be profitable to every Christian from any denomination and would enrich the life of every reader. The second book was; 'Strategic Spiritual Warfare' by Dr. Robert Ballard who excels in guiding and teaching how, and with what sort of weapons, we can wage spiritual warfare against the unseen enemy.

These books enriched my fledgling faith so much and pushed me on to surge forward and onward for Christ; that my mind may always be focused and aligned towards fulfilling God's purpose behind my creation.

I was in awe of the magnitude of their love, care and concern for struggling souls, like me and maybe even you, who can be considered a failure by our own family and people, who scrutinise our lives through their narrow lens of self-righteousness and judge us based on our past. As I have learned through Mama and Papa, if only we can see the potential that can be given to people through Christ, we would be less quick to judge.

The enemy of our soul does not give up, and as papa says, "As long as our spirit is contained in our body, weeds will seek to grow in our soul; but it is up to us to keep our garden right for the Master."

I have watched programmes where a child has never known their Mum or Dad and later in life, the child now being an adult, goes searching for their bloodline parent. Have you ever noticed, not only do they look somewhat alike but they can also have the same traits/ habits, and yet they never learned from being with each other, it was always in the genes? Every one of us will have some form of character trait passed down through our father and mother, whether good or bad. One of my character traits that I never noticed until later in life was, at certain times, I would drift away and get lost amidst the complex situations and recoil inside my shell - dejected and lonely, disconnecting from friends, family and from the outside world. In these times, I became like a loner but this trait must be overcome and broken over our lives, for the root cause is selfishness.

There were times – tough, difficult times, when I would spend hours thinking about my present state of affairs and my future, wondering if I would get a chance to tide over my past misadventures.

Deep in my remorse-filled nights, I would ponder on my problems, familial and personal, that I was beset with. When I realised that I had no solutions, I would be tempted to give up the fight. My unseen enemy would construct a platform out of all my ill-circumstances and proclaim my personal past failures while putting the onus of blame on me even for the current family problems...

"Just forget about the future; *you have no future.*"

"Just forget about your responsibilities; *its not worth your effort.*"

"The problems that have surfaced in your family are only a repercussion of *your failures.*"

"Just enjoy and live for the present and be gone."

"*You are a failure*, and it is given for failures to close the chapters of their lives and be gone."

My enemy would keep on barraging me with such lies after lies…; but, as difficult as my circumstances were, I never willed myself to follow the dictates of my enemy, and thus, in the silence of the night, I would bare my heart and my problems to God and plead for rescue.

During one such difficult time, I received a message from Mama telling me how much I was loved and desiring to know why I had gone silent.

When I narrated my problems to her she placed herself in 'the gap' (interceding) for me, and pleaded to God to kindly help me. Then gently she reined me back into her loving fold with understanding and grace. Mama then patiently and diligently started teaching me about the purpose behind God's immense love for me and urged me to stay In and With Love Himself.

CHAPTER 10

# *The Quill…*

I sent Mama a copy of my first attempt to publish a book, never thinking that my story would touch her so much. I was dumbstruck when she told me that it was now being considered for international publishing! In fact, you could have blown me over like a feather.

Wondering why God loved me so much Mama told me that it was because God had a purpose for me, and I should surrender to Him in order to fulfil that purpose. She told me that my story would help so many people; from those who are addicted, to those who have family members addicted, this would help them gain a greater understanding. Humbled and honoured, I gave my permission for the script to be published for international readership.

With the manuscript now submitted to an inspirational Christian publisher, a few weeks later Maurice Wylie Media returned it with suggestions, pin-pointing changes and to elaborate or strip it back where necessary.

Little did I realise that, what I thought was my book finished and printed initially was only a draft compared to the finished book that is now in your hand. I soon started on a new journey, revisiting my past and understanding better about God's love and purpose. As I began editing and scripting away, a life-changing book is born, it was as if I had an invisible quill in my hand as I wrote.

I was guided, prayed for, and always encouraged by Mama and Papa Maurice from the start of my latest venture till the last dot.

If you have got to this stage in the book, know it's because someone, from half a world away from me, dared and chose to follow the guiding star, revealed unto her in a vision, and never wavered in her faith to pursue it, even beyond the seas, till 'The star' finally led her to a lonely, desperate and struggling soul in a small, humble town in Nagaland the land where I was born. Just as God changed my life, He can change yours. He can take your mess and turn it into a message, a test into a testimony, if you will let Him.

Many who will be reading this book could be saying, like I said one time, "I am a druggie!" But being a druggie is what you do, it's not who you are! Let's change those words a little and can you say this... "Being a druggie is what I do, it's not who I am!"

You never started as a druggie in this life, so you do not have to end it as a druggie.

Let me tell you what you are... "You're a diamond of dust!"

Why would I say, "You're a diamond of dust?" It's quite simple... set a diamond into the middle of heroin, liquor, any other vice, and let me ask you... does the diamond reduce in value? The answer is NO!

The life I lived with drugs and alcohol was only penned to allow you to understand. Maybe there's someone you know, a son, daughter, or friend who is going through similar circumstances. It is also penned for the addict, allowing them to see the pain that comes with being just that, an addict.

'A Diamond of Dust' is an expression of my gratitude to the One and only One who was able to bring me out of the pit of abuse, where no other counsellor or treatment could.

Just as my reflection sometimes appears on the train window beside me, as I journey to my next engagement it's no longer the Anato that I told you about that needed cotton wool to fill his cheeks, this is the Anato that is on his journey home. That home is a destination, but let me explain...

Many will speak of one's home being bricks and mortar, but in truth, your home is when time meets destiny. That place where you can be alone but not lonely. That place where your heart is open and unafraid. That place where the visible meets the invisible, where your natural world meets the supernatural world of our Lord Jesus Christ.

Home my friend, is peace in our heart! And if our heart is secure in God, God is at home in our heart and that is the journey we are on... allowing the diamond to know the God who created it.

My Dad never saw the day when I, his son, would have made him proud, but in truth, I was always his son at the beginning and like the prodigal son in the Bible, (Luke 15) I have returned. What would I give for my Dad to see me now? My friend what I will give my Dad is one thing... he will see me in heaven where he awaits. We will spend eternity sharing how his seed of time and money, never got wasted but brought forth a harvest. The train in life is called, 'journey' the destination is Heaven for those who accept Jesus as their Lord.

I've found my way home in God, I pray you do too.

# One-Way, Second Chance Ride

My life is a one-way, second chance ride.
My destiny is what He makes me decide,
With the freewill to choose wrong or right,
And be of the dark world or with the Light.

I turn regrets into lessons I should learn.
The past is gone; I cannot make a U-turn,
And go back to reclaim all my lost years,
When I became the reason of much tears.

My ride's slow and bumpy; the road narrow;
I know not what awaits for me tomorrow;
Wind of adversity blows against my face,
That shan't deter me to keep up my pace.

Milestones of memories I leave behind.
Of the bitter past I choose not to rewind;
For what was done then, can't be undone.
What matters is now and it too will be gone!

Of the sharp bends of ugly circumstance,
That put my progress into a state of trance,
I know I can count on His Help and Grace,
And He alone shall let me finish this race!

Precious 'Diamond', if you would like to come to know the Almighty God as 'The God of the Second Chance' and 'The God of New Beginnings', and if you desire to know the Lord Jesus as your personal Saviour, then join me in the following prayer:

*Dear Jesus,*

*You know my heart today, like you have known my ways. You know my desires, my doubts, and my failure in becoming the person You want me to be.*

*I believe You died for my sin and conquered death by rising from the grave. Please forgive me for my sins and I invite You to come into my heart and life.*

*I accept Your gift of life and love, and realise that I am; 'A Diamond of Dust.'*

*Help me to come out from the dark confines of evil, and let me forever reflect You.*

*In Jesus' Name.*

*Amen.*

# Christ's 'Circle Of Friends'

*Behold Him, just as any other mortal human,*
*Cameth He to His footstool as a Son of man.*
*Walketh, eateth and worketh like a common being,*
*Forsaking the Heavenly abode where He'd been.*

*He could have had a council of wisemen,*
*Instead chooses him the lowly fisherman.*
*He could have been a friend of the emperor,*
*But preferred him the despised tax collector.*

*He could have earned the best of all the titles,*
*But more concerned was He for the Gentiles.*
*He could have the hypocrites stone the prostitute,*
*Instead He allowed her into His Heavenly institute.*

*Above all, He gave me a second chance to live,*
*Even though I had nothing of worth to give.*
*Indeed He brought me back from certain death,*
*Just because of His mercy and love, so great.*

*I was but once, the worst of all known abusers*
*Of drugs and alcohol that killeth my honour.*
*But no more do I crave for the worldly trend,*
*For Jesus Christ, I found, is my only true friend.*

- composed after making the covenant.

# *Guidelines*

Herein, I impart some 'Do's and Don'ts', based on my own experiences, to those parents and guardians who are concerned for their children's welfare in these unsafe environments, or are dealing with the menace of drugs or alcohol in their homes.

## *A.  General guidelines:*

1.  Arguments between parents are not uncommon. Nevertheless, try your best not to argue or quarrel in the presence of your children, particularly when they are in 'pick-up' or learning stage.

    Parental arguments often become stumbling blocks in the progress of the children by creating negativism in the family environment.

2.  Create time to be with them and be a good listener. Let your ward do most of the talking and observe any change in the accent or 'topic-jumping.' The latter indicates that something's not right.

    A silent listener always encourages the speaker and ofttimes offers the best shoulder to lean on.

3.  Appreciate and express delight in every bit of your ward's achievement. It could change that silver-lining into precious gold.

    Timely appreciation triggers the desire to pursue higher goals.

4.   Don't always poke your nose in your ward's affairs or bedroom (!) unless you suspect some foul play or sudden behavioural changes.

    Constant watch often leads to development of a negative sense of security.

5.   Don't be judgemental. Your verdict can lead to a lifetime condemnation when your intention was to just correct your ward as a parent.

    It is sometimes better to 'let go' and 'let God' work in their situation.

6.   Always keep your promises and let them be 'despite' instead of 'if.'

    Unfulfilled promises cause loss of trust and loss of confidence.

7.   Don't be over-protective. It could change a would-be leader into a follower among equals.

    Life's best lessons are often learned when left alone with nature. 'Nothing ventured, nothing gained.'

8.   Don't discuss financial problems in the presence of your ward when s/he is at the peak of study.

    Discuss economic values instead of financial setbacks.

9. Make dinner a family affair every day. Weave the fabric of love through small talk as you share the dishes. Encourage every member to talk about his/her day post-dinner.

   Shared love multiplies. Shared problem divides and becomes easier to solve.

10. Don't force your ward to do chores or study if your intuition tells you something's not normal. Be a friend and try to find out the source of the problem and nip it in the bud together.

    A parent is best when s/he becomes his/her ward's best friend.

11. Give your ward space and free time in solitude for self-introspection and self-growth, but count the minutes.

    Self-development begins with free time and space.

12. Conduct short family prayer meetings as much as you can and encourage everyone to share their hopes and dreams about 'the family's best future.'

    Group prayers are the building blocks of any good Christian family.

13. Appreciation is good and quite encouraging, but too much of it for a particular child can sow the seed of jealousy between siblings.

    Jealousy creates 'Josephism' among siblings and sparks hatred which destroys the love that binds a family.

## B.   *For those parents, whose ward(s) abuse drugs or suspect that they do.*

1.   Don't give money to your ward without getting a valid reason. If your confidence is established, then give away. If not, try to get his demands met by yourself.

Drug abusers usually have a sugar-coated tongue and can persuade others to part easily with their money or substances giving many excuses.

2.   Don't neglect when your ward starts skipping meals. Watch out for weight loss.

Most drug addicts usually suffer from loss of appetite and weight loss.

3.   Don't stop conversing with your ward, instead tell them, when s/he's in the mood of listening, just how much you love them but hate their habit and that God loves us but hates our sins.

Leaving a drug addict in their own world only encourages them to abuse drugs freely, often with deadly consequences.

4.   Don't ignore if you find syringes, empty gelatine capsules, silver foils, burnt matchsticks and cigarette butts in any part of the house. Confront them with your discovery when s/he is sober and warn them sternly, but don't give a lengthy lecture.

Drug addicts are always secretive but they often become careless and forgetful under the influence of drugs.

5.    Try playing the game 'whose nails are longer' with all the members of the family present. Ask each member to show his/her nails by turn. The one with the longest and dirtiest nails must forfeit. While playing, watch for any tremors; *the real purpose of the game.* If you find any, then get to the bottom of the cause and try to find the cure.

Normal, healthy people do not have tremors, whereas chronic drug abusers show signs of fine tremors in their stretched hands.

6.    Whenever your ward returns home late, ask them where they have been while quickly studying their eyes, mouth and accent. If their eyes are glazed and their mouth's parched, and they keep on looking away, don't say anything. Approach them only when they sober up. If they admit to their mistake, encourage them and tell them that they are not destined to take up such an evil habit to enjoy life.

Compulsive drug users become compulsive liars too.

7.    Don't curse, scold, lecture or preach when your ward is under the influence of any abusive substance. Try to let them rest/sleep off and deal with the matter only after they have rested or slept soundly.

Drug abuse changes perception and alters normal behaviour. Addicts are known to injure themselves and others too, over trivial matters and cases of suicide are not uncommon.

8.   Don't leave your ward behind bolted bathroom, toilet or even bedroom doors at odd hours, for more than the necessary period of time.

Intravenous Drug Users (I.V.D.U.) and brown sugar addicts often use the secrecy of toilet and bathrooms to administer the drug. I.V.D.U. deaths, due to overdose at such odd places have been reported.

9.   Try using the 4Gs (Gang of Good Guys & Girls) formula. Ask any group of good guys and girls from well bred families to help you with your ward's problem by requesting them to accept your ward in their 'circle of friends.'

In the company of good people, even the bad get a chance to become good.

10.  If you are trying to seek help medically, find out the best rehabilitation centre most suited for your ward's problem and not any other common centre that has popped up in many places. Don't force your ward to join any rehab, instead take time to encourage them and make effort to coax them out of their pre-conceived, reluctant mind.

Most cases of relapses occur among addicts who have been forced to join rehab centres by family members, without taking any consideration of their ward's interest.

If you want to get rid of your ward's addiction of any kind and for all time, then take them to any well-established prayer centre and seek God's intervention. Pray and fast together. Ask for the power of the Holy Spirit to break all the shackles of satan that is keeping your ward captive in his hands. Teach your ward how to pray for themselves if they haven't learned to do so. Prayers offered with a broken heart and contrite spirit gain easy access to God's help and mercy.

Problems of addiction may seem insurmountable but giving up is never an option. Take your burden to the Lord and allow Him to work in your life. He is ever-ready to listen and show you the easier and better way out.

# *Places of help*

*For more information of services in your own area:*
www.DrugsandAlcoholni.info (Northern Ireland)
www.NHS.uk (Great Britain)
www.HSE.ie (Ireland)

*Christian based support:*
www.TeenChallenge.org.uk
www.Betel.uk
www.VictoryOutreachUK.com
www.StaurosMinistries.com
www.CelebrateRecovery.co.uk
www.JoshuaProject.ie

~ o O o ~

To invite or contact the author email to
author@MauriceWylieMedia.com

MAURICE WYLIE MEDIA
*Inspirational Christian Publisher*
Based in Northern Ireland and distributing across the world.
www.MauriceWylieMedia.com

# FOOTNOTES

[1]    https://www.theguardian.com/society/2012/jun/26/global-drug-users-rise-un

[2]    https://www.northpointwashington.com/blog/percentage-population-struggles-addiction-answer-may-surprise

[3]    http://www.drugwise.org.uk/how-many-people-use-drugs

[4]    https://www.greenfacts.org/en/alcohol/l-2/01-number-people-affected

[5]    http://www.who.int/substance_abuse/publications/global_alcohol_report/msbgsruprofiles.pdf

[6]    Definition of 'Tribalism' from the online Cambridge English Dictionary, Cambridge University Press, https://dictionary.cambridge.org/dictionary/english/tribalism. Accessed June 2018. *Used by permission.*